I0712468

Just One Rodeo

The Billionaire Barons of Texas — Book Ten

CHRIS KENISTON

Indie House Publishing

Indie House Publishing

MORE BOOKS
By Chris Keniston

The Billionaire Barons of Texas
Just One Date
Just One Spark
Just One Dance
Just One Take
Just One Taste
Just One Shot
Just One Chance
Just One Mistake
Just One Family
Just One Rodeo
Just One Surprise
Just One Look

Hart Land
Heather
Lily
Violet
Iris
Hyacinth
Rose
Calytrix
Zinnia
Poppy
Picture Perfect

Farraday Country
Adam
Brooks
Connor
Declan
Ethan

Finn
Grace
Hannah
Ian
Jamison
Keeping Eileen
Loving Chloe
Morgan
Neil
Owen
Paxton

Honeymoon Series
Honeymoon for One
Honeymoon for Three
Honeymoon for Four
Honeymoon for Five
Honeymoon for Six
Honeymoon for Seven

Aloha Romance Series:
Aloha Texas
Almost Paradise
Mai Tai Marriage
Dive Into You
Look of Love
Love by Design
Love Walks In
Shell Game
Flirting with Paradise

Surf's Up Flirts:
(Aloha Series Companions)
Shall We Dance
Love on Tap
Head Over Heels
Perfect Match
Just One Kiss
It Had to Be You
Cat's Meow

CHAPTER ONE

"It's time!" Claire Baron's vet tech shouted from the hallway.

Checking on one of her post-op patients still sleeping off the anesthesia, Claire gave the sweet cattle dog a pat on the head and strolled over to the doorway. She was positive she'd canceled all morning appointments for the emergency surgery, and couldn't figure what the woman was shouting about. Sticking her head into the hall, she looked for her tech. "Time for what?"

"For what?" Kathy came hurrying down the hall from the front, grinning wider than a lottery winner. "The baby!"

Baby. Claire blinked and then recognition dawned. So consumed with the injured dog, she'd forgotten the entire family was on baby watch for her cousin Mitch and his wife. "How long has she been in labor?" Claire slipped out of her lab coat and quickly hung it on a nearby hook.

"Rachel didn't tell me."

Claire hurried down the hall to her office, Kathy right on her heels. "What about the contractions? How far apart are they?"

Kathy shook her head. "I don't know."

Grabbing her purse from the desk drawer, Claire leveled her gaze with Kathy. "Water broke?"

Shoulders lifted in a shrug at the same time Kathy's hands flipped up in an *I don't know* gesture.

Biting back her frustration at limited information, Claire slammed the drawer shut and smiled up at Kathy. "What exactly did Rachel say?"

"Gwyneth is in labor and your presence has been requested at the ranch ASAP."

Her purse slung over her shoulder, Claire gave up digging for her truck keys and snapped her head up. "Me? Why me?"

"You are a medical professional." Kathy shrugged again.

"Yeah, for four-legged critters, not humans. I don't do humans."

Kathy chuckled. "Relax. It sounds like the call went out far and wide. If it makes you feel any better, Rachel mentioned that CJ was already on the way."

That did help. A trained nurse, CJ would be way more helpful in this situation than Claire would. "Okay. I know first babies are notoriously slow, but since we have no idea if she's been laboring for ten minutes or ten hours, I'm heading out to the ranch as summoned. When Gail comes back from lunch, tell her to cancel the remainder of my appointments for the day."

"Will do." Kathy nodded. "And please keep us posted."

"Deal." Hurrying back up the hall, she suddenly remembered her post-op patient and, stuttering to a stop, spun about. "The dog."

Kathy waved her back around. "Go. I'll keep an extra eye on him. Even sleep with him if I have to. Just don't forget to call with updates." Kathy's hands fisted in front of her and she practically shook with excitement. "This is so much fun. We're having a baby!"

Something told Claire that if it were Kathy having the baby, she wouldn't use the word fun.

Pushing the pedal to the metal, Claire turned on the music and picked her favorite artist, blaring full blast. They were having a baby. The first in the family. She was so darn excited anyone would think it was Claire or one of her sisters who was about to become a mother. Gwyneth had only been a Baron for a little more than a year, but it felt like she'd always been part of the family, making this event so exciting for everyone. After all, Gwyneth wasn't laboring at her and Mitch's house. She'd decided against the midwife's birthing center at the hospital, wanting to have the baby in the comfort of a home. Mitch had insisted on having her surrounded by family and Gwyneth was all for giving birth at the ranch. Another example of how the woman had embraced being a Baron.

At the same time Claire pulled onto the property, a line of cars pulled in behind her, adding to the row of cars already parked along the curved drive. Apparently, the entire clan had indeed been called.

Inside, siblings and cousins were scattered about. Some in the living room seated, others pacing, others in the kitchen making sandwiches and coffee with Hazel. The excitement was running so high that the air almost crackled with it.

"How long has she been in labor?" Claire addressed the women in the kitchen.

Hazel flipped her wrist. "We think her back ache last night was the beginning. Gwyneth woke up this morning grumbling and disinterested in breakfast. That's when I knew."

"When did she know?" Claire asked.

Hazel shrugged. "When I told her. We called the doula right away. She's upstairs with the midwife."

Rubbing her hands together, Claire joined the pacers in the living room. Now all she had to do was hurry up and wait.

Spectators filled the towering grandstands in the dusty small-town arena. The scents of leather and hay mingled with the faint aroma of barbecue drifting in from the nearby concessions. For Tucker, all of it smelled like heaven. Slapping his hat on his thigh and placing it back on his head, he took a quick glance around. He didn't have to hear the rising hum of voices to know the air was thick with anticipation for tonight's events—he could feel it all around him like a warm blanket. Right along with an edge of excitement, just enough to have him and his best horse, Thunder, eager to nail this last event. After another long year on the circuit, if he and Sam could keep up the points for the next couple of events, they'd have what they needed to make it to the grand national finals and the top prize he'd coveted all season. The purse he needed to make all he'd worked for and dreamed about a reality.

Tucker glanced over at his longtime friend and partner in team roping. Sam reminded him of the stereotypical cowboy. His face rugged with weathered features, and a perpetual twinkle in his eye. The man's easy smile belied the years of hard work and dedication he'd poured into the rodeo circuit. This would be their year. Tucker could feel it in his bones, right alongside every bump and bruise. Thunder was the best damn horse a man could ask for, and Sam's horse Gray was a close second.

His Stetson pulled low over his brow as he surveyed the scene before them, Sam bobbed his head and sported a lazy, contented smile. "You ready to take this home?"

Tucker nodded. "More than ready. All we have to do is stay on our horses and we're in like Flynn."

Sam snorted a knowing chuckle, as if either of them would fall off a horse that wasn't bucking.

Coming toward them, a man and two young boys focused on Tucker and Thunder. When they were close enough to hear the conversation over the hum of the crowds, one kid spat *it's him,* and the other hollered back, *is not.* The bickering brothers made him smile, remembering the same one-upmanship between him and his brother. In the end, the father leaned over, nodded, and must have uttered the magic words because both boys looked thoroughly reproved and appropriately contrite. As they walked by, one raised his head and his thumb. "We're rooting for you, Tucker. You and Thunder."

"Much obliged." He tipped his hat to the boys. Still a bit startled whenever someone recognized him, or, like the boys, actually followed his career. The whole concept of being well known in the circuit caught him off guard every time.

As a young boy, he'd followed his favorite rodeo riders and dreamed of the day he could win the buckle himself.

After all, at the age of six, what boy cared about money? It was the shiny buckle that held his dreams. Some days he couldn't believe his life had become a dream come true. At least that would be the case if the finals went as well as this season. Too many other days, he awoke with the standard aches and pains and knew his days on the circuit were numbered. This *had* to be his year.

He carefully watched the team in the arena do their thing. A late start here or a missed rope toss there, Tucker knew all too well how much the slightest misstep could cost in the rankings.

Mounted and ready for their turn, their hats pulled low over their brows, Tucker and Sam guided their horses into position on either side of the steer's gate. Tucker's grip tightened on the reins, his gaze locked on the pen where the animals waited. Sam exuded calm confidence and focused concentration as he readied his rope, set to ride like the proverbial wind.

Tucker felt a surge of adrenaline course through his veins as the announcer's voice boomed over the loudspeaker, signaling the start of their run. This was their moment, their chance to shine beneath the bright lights of the rodeo arena. Tucker urged Thunder forward, the powerful horse surging into action with effortless grace. The wind whipped around Tucker as they thundered across the arena, the rhythm of Thunder's hooves echoing in perfect sync with the pounding of Tucker's heart.

In the blink of an eye, they closed in on their target—a lone steer racing ahead. Focused on the task at hand, Tucker's pulse quickened, his senses sharpening with each passing second. With practiced precision, Sam expertly wielded his lasso, the rope whirling overhead before settling around the steer's horns with pinpoint accuracy. The steer kicked its rear legs, twisting around, its movements tempered by the ropes that bound it.

Tucker's breath came in exhilarated gasps as he swung his rope, the loop sailing through the air in a graceful arc before settling around the steer's hind legs. A chorus of cheers erupted from the crowd. With the steer now securely roped at both ends, Tucker and Sam exchanged a knowing glance, a silent acknowledgment of their synchronized skill and unwavering teamwork. Needed points secured, he bobbed his head, loosening his grip on the ropes and letting the steer hurry away. They'd done it. Their fastest time of the evening. One step closer to finals, he knew they'd make it as surely as he knew his name was Tucker John Pride.

CHAPTER TWO

"Isn't she the most beautiful baby you've ever seen?" Standing over the lacey bassinet, Claire cooed at the sleeping little Elizabeth Marie Baron.

"Of course she is." Lila Baron patted the swaddled baby's side and directed all the ogling relatives to leave the nursery. Having raised six children of her own and participated in the upbringing of a couple dozen grandchildren, Grams was the resident baby expert. In the few weeks since little Beth had been born, Grams had proven herself more of an authority on infants than the nurse Mitch had hired.

Halfway down the hall, the older woman shook her head. "Frankly, you young people have it too easy. We had to fold our own diapers, try not to scream every time we jabbed our fingers with a pin, and redo the wrapped blankets when the baby squirmed out of it. These newfangled swaddles with Velcro are the best invention since pantyhose."

"Pantyhose, not disposable diapers?" Gwyneth followed Grams down the stairs.

Grams shrugged. "Infants are only in diapers for a short time. Women, on the other hand, had to wear a girdle with stockings all the time until some wonderful person invented pantyhose."

To this day, when modern women had left wearing pantyhose by the wayside, her grandmother was always properly dressed, stockings and all. A lesson she'd learned from her mother. According to family lore, a fire had started early one morning and Grams had been carried outside to safety. When the firemen arrived and asked if everyone was safely out of the house, they realized that Grams' mother was nowhere outside. The woman had gone back into the house, put on her makeup, her girdle, and was clipping her stockings when the firemen were forced to wrap her in a blanket and carry her out. Apparently, she had refused to leave the house until she was properly dressed.

"I'm surprised she went down so easily." Gwyneth flopped into the oversized club chair. "She doesn't seem to be eating very well."

"Really?"

"It's like she's not interested."

"I see." Quietly, Grams left the room and returned with a small silver tray, one bottle of beer, and a frosted glass. "Drink this."

At the horrified look on Gwyneth's face, Claire had to stifle a laugh.

"Thank you, Grams, but I'm not very fond of beer." Gwyneth smiled demurely.

Her grandmother shook her head. "Doesn't matter. It's good for you and the baby will eat more."

Cooper, who had been sitting in the chair opposite Gwyneth, looked up at his grandmother. "A little young to be learning to hold her liquor, don't you think?"

The look their grandmother shot him could wither an oak tree. "Watch it."

Even more amused by her brother's foolish teasing, Claire nodded. "Grams is right. Of course. It's the brewer's yeast." She turned to face Gwyneth. "If you don't like beer, they sell an awful lot of products from cookies to shakes that have brewer's yeast and are specifically designed for nursing mothers."

Beer glass in hand, staring down at it as though it were arsenic, like a trooper, Gwyneth took a long sip and swallowed before facing Claire. "I'll get on that right away. Thank you."

The alarm on her phone buzzed and Claire pushed to her feet. "As much as I'd like to stay, I'm replacing Doc Jordan at the rodeo today."

"I thought the rodeos don't start till later in the day?"

Devlin looked to his sister.

"Unless you're a cowboy or a veterinarian. We need to be there long before the crowds."

He nodded. "Makes sense. Don't get stomped on."

"Ha ha." She did her best to shoot him the same withering glare her grandmother had used, but she was pretty sure she'd totally failed to pull it off.

Just an hour north of the ranch, she pulled into the back lot behind the arena. Horse trailers and quad cabs parked every which way used up every available inch of parking. Thankfully, the veterinarian was important enough to have a designated parking space; otherwise she might be parking out in the boondocks.

The moment she passed through the doorway into the rear of the arena, the familiar scents of hay, leather, and horse manure smacked her in the face. She really must be crazy, but she truly loved the combination. Even the manure brought back sweet memories of her childhood on the ranch. Soon the smell of barbecue and popcorn would be added to the mix.

One of these days she was going to attend a rodeo where they served lasagna or sushi. Although she doubted the Texas tradition of pulled pork and brisket would ever be replaced. Corn on the cob, fried okra, and cole slaw were an equally important food staple on the circuit. Probably had been since the days of the Wild West.

"I'm sorry, miss. This is a restricted area."

"Yes." Reaching into her bag, she pulled out the lanyard with the ID card that Doc Jordan had given her. "I'm the vet today."

Frowning, the man looked down at her badge and up at her face. Nodding, he seemed more resigned than pleased. "You any good with kids? Doc Jordan is."

It took her a moment to realize the man wasn't talking about young goats. "I like them. Does that count?"

"One of the kids fell and hurt his ankle. We've been waiting for Doc."

"I'm not a people doctor. The parents should take him to an urgent care."

The man shook his head. "Dad's in the rodeo, mom is home. Doc would fix it."

Doc. Like it or not, it looked like she was about to do people. "Lead the way."

Points earned earlier this evening had secured Tucker's place in the finals, but they still had two more rounds scheduled before the finalists were officially announced, and every additional point earned would secure their standings in the ranks. With a final pat on Thunder's flank, Tucker mounted his horse. His grip firm on the reins, he guided Thunder into position as they waited for their turn in the arena. Sam stood on the other side of the penned steer. The moment they'd waited for was upon them. The announcer's voice boomed over the loudspeaker, signaling their turn to compete. Thunder danced beneath him, knowing it was their turn next, and Tucker deliberately loosened his grip on the reins.

His pulse quickened with anticipation. The gate opened and the steer bolted forward out of the pen. Tucker let Thunder go. The powerful horse surged into action with effortless grace. The crowd's cheers faded into the background as they thundered across the arena, intent on stopping the moving steer.

As expected, Sam's rope flew through the air and easily slid over the steer's horns, stopping the animal's race across the arena. Determined to break itself free, the steer kicked and twisted with more fervor than most, but nothing Tucker couldn't handle. Tucker's rope twirled high, ready to fly when the steer unexpectedly twisted in the opposite direction. The minute the steer spun away, Thunder twisted, trying to follow, and took an off step. When Thunder jerked his neck up and did a weird little hop, Tucker knew something had happened. Dismounting faster than he'd thought possible, he gently patted his heaving horse.

Sam had already dropped down from his mount and was

at Tucker's side. "How bad is it?"

Tucker was almost afraid to look. Sure enough, his worst fear. A deep laceration on Thunder's hoof had blood staining the ground beneath him. "Damn."

Picking the hoof up, he ran his fingers over the bloody spot. Thunder jerked when he found the slice. "It's okay, buddy," Tucker soothed. Ripping his red kerchief from his neck, he wrapped it around the hoof to give the cut some support. Sam shoved his own kerchief toward Tucker, and he wrapped it around the hoof as well. The less dirt in the cut the better.

The entire arena seemed to be holding their breath. Several of the arena hands had dismounted as well in an effort to help.

"Get the doc!" one had yelled.

"We need to get him out of here!" another called.

Carefully and slowly, Tucker guided the horse out of the arena and harm's way, toward their designated stalls. The crowd stood applauding Thunder's ability to limp off on his own steam. Worst-case scenarios paraded across Tucker's thoughts. Finals be damned, Thunder was his best friend. Nothing could happen to him. It just couldn't.

Whispering comforting words to the animal as they stepped into their stall, Tucker prayed it wasn't as serious as he suspected. "Where's the doc?"

"Coming," one of the hands tried to reassure.

Tucker stripped off Thunder's tack, dumping the expensive saddle to the side in a heap. Then he stripped off the bridle, tossing it aside, and replaced it with the soft halter Sam handed him. "Yeah, buddy, does that feel better? We'll get you fixed up."

A moment later a tall blonde with her hair tied back in a ponytail and wearing a hat that probably cost more than his first car came walking into the stall.

"Sorry, ma'am, but this area is off limits." He needed curious bystanders like he needed a hole in his head.

She came to a sudden stop. "Excuse me?"

"No offense, but spectators are not allowed back here."

"Yes. I'm aware." The woman showed no signs of

moving. As a matter of fact, the way she stared at him, he better understood the expression stared daggers. "Your horse is hurt."

Oh great, vicious stares and the queen of understatement. Just the kind of snoopy rodeo fan he did not need right about now. "You really need to leave now, ma'am. We're waiting on the doc, and you shouldn't be back here." For just a second as she blinked tightly at him, he wondered if he was going to have to call security or personally escort her out of the participants stables.

"I'll have you know…" With one hand fisted on her hip and one booted foot tapping heavily—like with the hat, a very expensive boot—she looked just a fragment more menacing than she had a moment ago.

"Here you go, Doc." One of the men who had been working the arena handed her a large black bag. "This what you wanted?"

The woman nodded, her smile—in direct contrast to the glare she'd shot Tucker's way—softened her eyes. "Thanks. I'll let you know if I need anything else out of my truck."

"Doc?" Tucker repeated.

"As in, the veterinarian who is going to tend to your horse's hoof. Unless, of course, you still think this area is off limits to me?"

"No, ma'am." He shook his head, wondering how hard it would be to eat his size thirteen boots.

"Good. Then get out of my way."

"Thunder doesn't like strangers."

"Thunder doesn't have a choice right now." Her bag on the ground, she took a step closer to his best horse and spoke in a more soothing tone. "How's my boy feeling?"

To Tucker's surprise, rather than shoving her away or nipping, the horse shook his head and moved his lips.

"Oh, I'm sorry, boy." She inched closer, her hand gently caressing Thunder's jaw. "We're going to fix you up and make you feel better. Does that sound good?"

The beast that usually bit people he didn't know bobbed his head at her. What the heck?

"Give me a minute, we'll see how bad this is." The

woman gently rubbed her hands along Thunder's shoulder, and before he'd even noticed, she'd injected him with a sedative. Then she eased her way toward the injured leg. With coos and reassurances, she had his injured leg in her hands, working quickly and carefully to remove the kerchiefs and evaluate the issue. His only hint to the severity of the situation was a slow tightening of her lips followed by a heavy exhale.

Reaching for the bucket of clean water someone set beside her, she splashed the injury, washing away sawdust and dirt. Then Tucker saw the cut down the bulb of Thunder's heel, just above the hoof. Hell. That was a bad place to repair.

The bulb was a tough, spongy area that cushioned the horse's foot at the back. When it absorbed the weight from a footstep, it expanded.

"I saw the steer zigzag," the woman said, reaching for her bag. "And I think Thunder here might have clipped his front hoof with his back hoof when he changed leads to follow."

"He's never clipped his own feet before," Tucker said.

"He did this time."

Tucker watched as she reached for a syringe. Thunder barely moved as she started injecting pain medication around the cut. "Somebody get me a feed sack."

Within seconds, a feed sack was shoved toward her. She straightened the sack, then set Thunder's hoof down on it, keeping it out of the dirt. The hoof was still bleeding, but it had eased a little.

Pushing to her feet, she patted the horse's side and looked over to him.

"Besides being a chauvinist, would you be his owner?"

Chauvinist wasn't a word he heard very often, and the mere suggestion had him ready to snort and stamp his feet. Instead, he settled for a short nod and civil words. "Thunder is my horse."

"Where is home base for you two?"

That wasn't the kind of question he'd expected. "Here, there and a little bit of everywhere."

"How far is a little bit of everywhere?"

He had to think for a minute; if he needed a place to stay and tend to Thunder longer term, that would have to be Rick's place. "Wyoming."

The way she sucked in a whistled breath told him that was not what she'd wanted to hear. Blowing out another one of those heavy exhales, she shook her head. "The sedative has kicked in, so I'm going to stitch up that bulb when it's numb. We need to get him settled in a stall sooner than later. He needs to get off that foot. Be able to lay down. That much travel in a trailer will only make things worse. He's going to be in a lot of pain." She scratched under the horse's jaw again and for the first time, her gaze held no animosity. "We'll take him to my grandfather's. It's less than an hour's trailer ride and we can get him settled and well tended to."

"I tend to Thunder."

Her head bobbed. "Good to hear. Between all of us, we'll have him up and his old self in no time at all."

"How long is no time?"

Another one of those exhales grated against his nerves like nails on a chalkboard.

"If it's not as bad as I think, a few weeks. More likely, a couple of months. That area expands a lot, so keeping the stitches in and healing is going to be a challenge. At the very least, he's going to be wearing a pressure boot to keep it secure."

Months? His mind ran through his bank accounts and boarding costs. "I, uh, don't have—"

Before he could finish his sentence, her hand was up and she was shaking her head at him. "We're taking him to Paradise Ridge. You can come if you like, or you can go here, there or everywhere and I'll let you know when he can be moved again."

"That horse doesn't go anywhere without me."

For a second, he thought he saw a hint of a smile tease at her tight lips, and flash in her eyes. "Good. Give me a little bit, then we'll get on the road."

She turned back to the horse and started probing the

hoof, making sure it was numb. Then she laid out stitching supplies.

Tucker watched as she put six heavy-duty stitches into the bulb of Thunder's hoof. By the time she was done, it had stopped bleeding and looked secure.

"Somebody run out to my truck," she huffed. "Passenger side bed box, left-hand side. Get me the black Easyboot."

A nearby rodeo hand took off running. The vet bandaged the hoof, running yards of dressing around it, then elastic vet wrap. When they brought the boot, she fitted it over everything, then set his hoof down on the bag. She made sure the hoof sat in the boot correctly before fastening the metal clip on the front, tightening the cables on the sides of the boot, and securing it to the hoof.

On her feet again, she brushed her hair from her flushed face. "Let's get him loaded up. I'll be able to leave in about thirty minutes and we'll get Thunder settled in."

Had it been about himself, he would have argued from now till dooms day – but for Thunder, he'd sleep under a bridge, and beg for food. Scratching his horse's neck, Tucker wondered if her grandfather's place had any good bridges nearby.

CHAPTER THREE

aving called ahead to the ranch, Mack had prepared a nice clean stall for their visitor. A sanctuary for the injured animal. The horse's owner had been following on her tail ever since they'd left the arena. She was pretty sure if the guy could have crawled into the trailer with his horse, he would have. While she wasn't overjoyed with his attitude, she'd filled in for Doc Jordan at the rodeos often enough to know there was always one cowboy who doubted she could do the job simply because she didn't have a Y chromosome. In this case, she did, however, admire Mr. Chauvinist's devotion to Thunder.

Not that the relationship was that unusual between a cowboy and a good cow horse, but some men were just jerks. Heaven knew she's run into more than her share in the recent past.

Rather than stop at the house to greet her grandparents as she normally would, she drove directly to the stables and pulled up far enough away to leave room for Tucker to park his truck and the horse trailer near the entry doors.

Hopping out of her truck, she hurried over to meet Tucker by the trailer.

The man was already unfastening the back gate. "You'd better let me get him out. I suspect by now he's going to be awfully skittish."

She nodded. Anything to make the transition easier on the poor animal.

Inside, the injured horse waited patiently, its gentle whinnies echoing in the confined space. With steady hands, he slipped beside the horse, untying the lead rope. "It's all right, Thunder. This nice doc is going to take good care of you."

The horse regarded them with wary eyes, its body tense with pain and apprehension. Nothing about the horse told Claire that he believed a word Tucker had just said. The horse's ears flickered and he backed up a step.

Following her gut, the same as she'd done since long before graduating from vet school, she inched toward the trailer, pausing at Tucker's side. "Let me try."

Tucker shook his head. "He doesn't cotton to strangers."

The horse glared at him and then snorted. Whether Thunder was agreeing or disagreeing was anyone's guess.

"It's all right. I'll wait here, boy." She took a step back. "You are a handsome fellow, aren't you?"

The horse seemed to consider her words before lowering his head and letting Tucker back him out. Taking a moment, Tucker scratched at the horse's jaw. The pain in the cowboy's eyes seemed as deep as the horse's physical pain.

"That's a nice fellow," she uttered softly as Tucker led him forward, his touch light and reassuring as they made their way down the ramp. Thunder favored the injured hoof, but he was using it, telling her the medication was still working.

With each step, Tucker spoke to the horse in soothing tones, his voice a steady presence amidst the quiet of the stables. Thunder's tension began to ease with each passing moment. "Which way?" Tucker looked over his shoulder at her.

Mack, the family's longtime foreman, came hurrying out to meet them. "This way."

Slowly and carefully, they followed Mack to the prepared stall.

Taking in the horse's demeanor, Claire looked at Tucker. "I need to evaluate the bandage. You'd better stay close, keep him calm and steady. I'd rather not take a kick to the chest."

Tucker nodded. His arm gently around the horse's neck,

he stood so Thunder wouldn't see what she was doing. Smart man.

Crouching low, she popped off the Easyboot. There was no blood on the bandage, so she replaced the boot. He'd shipped well.

She pushed to her feet, content with her handiwork. "It looks good."

Tucker moved aside as she stretched. "Thank you." His gaze scanned the massive barn. "I, uh, have some money saved."

"That's not important now. The important thing is getting Thunder well."

"Will he be able to make the finals?"

Wouldn't she like to know.

Tucker had no idea how he was going to pay for Thunder's treatment, but one thing he was sure of, a place like this, the horse was going to get the best possible care. He supposed this wouldn't be the first or last time he bunked in the cab of his truck. All he needed was some place to shower and he could make do. Especially since he had every intention of sticking with Thunder.

"I will, of course, take an X-ray to make sure there are no broken bones, but the cut alone will take weeks. Depending upon how quickly the sutures heal, even if he improves by then, I wouldn't expect a winning performance out of him."

That was what he was afraid she was going to say.

"Don't get me wrong. The wound is bad, but it's not the worst I've ever seen. It's just prone to infection. The hoof is a dirty, moist area, and things like to grow there. Still, if you want to make the finals—"

"We've already qualified," he interrupted.

The way her brows arched momentarily high on her forehead, she seemed to understand how unusual that was. "I see. Regardless, if you intend to participate, you'll probably want a different horse."

Different horse? He held back the deep sigh that threatened to choke him. Thunder was the best cow horse he'd ever had the privilege to ride. Today was the perfect example. When the steer twisted away, without any guidance from him, Thunder made the lead change on his own like any good natural cow horse. The second Thunder misstepped, Tucker knew it, felt it. And hated that his horse hurt.

Washing her hands at the nearby sink, the doc dried them and turned to face him. "For now. Follow me to the house. Hazel will fix you up something warm to eat."

As if his stomach understood English, it chose that very moment to rumble. He never liked to eat before an event, and under normal circumstances, by now he and Sam would be enjoying a cool beer after a hot dinner. Before he'd managed to pull his thoughts and a response together, the doc—whose name he didn't even know—had turned away and was marching up the lawn toward the big white house.

Though *house* was what many would call an understatement. The place appeared big enough for a resort hotel. No matter how many purses he won, he'd never be in the same league as this place. What he really wanted right now was a chance to shower and change; his dust covered denims weren't exactly a high-class fashion statement, and he wasn't even going to mention that he most likely smelled of hay and leather and lord knew what else. Slapping his hat against his thigh and running his fingers through his hair would have to do.

"Evening, Hazel."

Standing at the kitchen sink, an older woman with a smile that could sell hair tonic to a bald man, stepped back, dried her hands and shoved one in his direction. "You must be the man with an injured horse. Nice to meet you."

"Likewise. Tucker Pride."

The older woman's eyes widened just enough to hint at recognition. "Please don't tell me Thunder is the injured horse?"

"I'm afraid so."

Her face fell. "Poor baby."

"You're a rodeo fan?" Way to go, Tucker, ask a stupid question.

"Yes, sir." She perked up. "Saw you at the Houston Rodeo earlier this year. What a horse."

"Agreed." He smiled.

Her face turned a bright shade of pink. "Oh, dear. Of course, you were excellent too."

That made him smile. "Thank you."

"If you'll go ahead and join the Governor and Miss Lila in the dining room, I'll bring out some hot food."

"Oh, good." The doc slapped her hands together. "They haven't finished supper."

"No, Miss Claire. They waited until they heard your truck pull in to have dinner served."

Claire. At least now he knew the doc's name. But Governor? For his sake he sure hoped they were British and it was a nickname.

"There you are." Seated at one end of a massive dining room table, a sweet-looking woman smiled at the doc.

The doc hugged the woman first, then circled the table to kiss the man at the opposite end on the cheek. In between there were several hellos, and how is it going by at least a dozen people seated around the table. Maybe this place really was a hotel.

"Welcome." The older man motioned for him to take a seat.

Claire made quick introductions, but the only two words that stood out were Governor and Senator. Tucker nodded and smiled, and as his brain connected the dots, he did his best not to hyperventilate. They were not British, they were Texas Royalty. Holy cow. What the heck was he doing here, so very far out of his doublewide comfort zone?

"Very sorry to hear about your horse," The Governor's tone dripped with sincerity, the same as any ordinary man might say.

"Not just any horse." Hazel stood beside him holding a large silver tray with two plated dishes. "This is Tucker Pride and you've got Thunder in your stable."

Unlike Hazel, the name clearly meant nothing to the older man.

"Makes no never mind who the horse is. In this house, every creature is treated the same."

Judging by the way the large cattle dog sat against his master, happily having the back of his neck rubbed, Tucker felt confident that treatment would be stellar.

"He's going to be here a bit." Claire took a seat beside where the man had directed him to sit. "I'll be checking on him regularly. The bandage will have to be changed daily."

"Though I'm sorry about the horse's injuries," her grandmother shook her head at Claire, "we're always delighted to see more of you."

"And you, young man," the Governor cleared his throat, "I suppose you'll be wanting to stay near your horse as well?"

He nodded, while under the table, wiping his sweaty palms on his jeans. "Yes, sir."

"Very well. The bunkhouse for our staff is full, but if it's to your liking, we have space at the visitor's quarters."

Had he ever known a ranch to have a visitor's bunkhouse?

"If that's not suitable—" the older woman started.

"No, ma'am. That will be just fine, I'm sure." Considering up until a few minutes ago, he was planning on sleeping in his truck, pretty much anything else would be palatial. Though looking around this place, he had a feeling even the dog house would be fit for a king. How lucky could one man… and horse…get?

CHAPTER FOUR

The clock was ticking, dinner was delicious as usual, but Claire wanted to check on her newest patient. Thunder was a stunning horse and she could so easily see the unease in his eyes.

"What's the prognosis?" Mitch reached for his coffee cup with one hand, and patted his wife beside him with the other.

"Cut heel bulb. He clipped his front hoof with his rear."

Mitch and Devlin both nodded. They were the two horsemen in the family. Though his work in Washington kept him quite busy, Mitch still participated heavily in the ranching side of the family. Especially since his marriage to Gwyneth. Devlin, on the other hand, had been a junior national rodeo champ in his youth and had continued to occasionally participate on an amateur level until real estate consumed all his waking hours. For now, the stern set of their jaws meant they understood the implications for Tucker.

"Do you have plans for the rest of the season?" Mitch asked.

Tucker shook his head.

His gaze narrowed and his lips pressed into a thin line, Devlin bobbed his chin and began fidgeting with a nearby spoon. "Do you have another horse?"

Pushing the food around on his plate, Tucker shook his head. "Thunder is a hard horse to beat."

"So I've heard." Devlin glanced down at the spoon and then back up. "According to Hazel, you and Thunder are the closest thing to perfection in the arena."

"Every so often a rider is blessed to have a horse that

instinctively does all you want and more. Thunder is that horse."

Porter looked to his cousin Devlin. "Sounds a lot like Star."

"You know," Claire nodded, "they do both have that look of eagles."

"Look of eagles?" For the first time since sitting beside her, Tucker turned to face her.

"I believe the special horses, the ones born to win, have a common look in their eyes. I've always called it the look of eagles."

"Really?" Tucker seemed to consider her words.

"On the other hand." Devlin chuckled. "Don't let my sister bamboozle you. She got that from an old black and white film set in race horse country in the 1940s."

"Doesn't matter where I first heard it. I believe it. And," she leaned forward and shot her brother a don't-argue-with-me glare, "I've seen it."

"Is Star your horse?" Tucker addressed Porter.

"Nope." Porter waved his thumb over his shoulder, pointing at Devlin. "I can ride like every Baron on this ranch, but my dear cousin is the one who could have done the pro-rodeo circuit if he hadn't wanted to be a real estate mogul instead."

"And Star was the horse that would have made it happen." The Governor appeared to address Porter and Tucker, but his gaze was fixed on Devlin.

At this point, Claire was catching on to what some of the men were thinking. "Do you think he can still do it?"

Devlin shrugged. "I know he would love to have a chance."

"He does seem a bit restless some days," Mitch agreed with the others.

Tucker followed the conversation like a spectator at a tennis match.

"I take him out through the paces sometimes, but it's not the same." Mitch looked to Devlin.

"I know." Devlin sighed. "I've tried the same, but I can't help but feel he's never been quite happy with me for retiring him."

"I think it's a great idea." The Governor turned to Tucker. "Don't you?"

Tucker looked at the Governor, then skipped to each of the men at the table before looking back. "Am I understanding that you want me to ride your horse in the national finals?"

"You've got, what, three, four weeks." Claire shifted in her seat to face Tucker. "If you're as good as Hazel says, and I know how good Star is, it can be done."

Dark brows folded over his eyes, Tucker considered her words a long moment before turning to Devlin. "How long since he's ridden in a contest arena?"

"Seven years," Devlin shot out without hesitation. "He's still got it in him."

What Claire couldn't determine was if Tucker's silence was buying him time to find a polite way to tell them hell no, or if he was debating if this was a viable solution to his current ambitions.

"Why don't you settle into your room," Grams dabbed at each corner of her mouth with her napkin, "and then one of the boys can introduce you to Star."

"Yes, ma'am. Thank you. That's an excellent idea."

For the first time all evening, the man actually smiled. His entire face seemed to change. Dark blue eyes that had been dim with worry now held a flicker of light. She could imagine all the buckle bunnies falling at his feet when he flashed that perfect smile. With her luck, he probably knew a smile and a belt buckle would get Mr. Chauvinist anything he wanted. Well, not from this gal. No way did she have room for another jerk in her life.

More than once in his lifetime, Tucker had shared a bunkhouse with other hands. Working on a ranch was a common way to earn a living early in his rodeo career, or to pad the coffers off-season. Dropping his belongings he'd retrieved from the truck on a nearby chair, he scanned the small space. Beyond the shadow of any doubt, he had never stayed in a bunkhouse quite like this. He wasn't even sure if it was correct to call the place a bunkhouse. What had they called it? Guest quarters? For starters, there was no shared space with bunks lined along the walls and a single shower space the way folks would expect to find in a dormitory. Nope. Each hand had their own room, with their own bath, and even a small kitchenette area with a microwave, mini fridge and two burner hot plate. By an ordinary cow hand's standard, this was the lap of luxury.

"You should find everything you need in here." Mitch opened a cabinet door that contained sheets and towels and a fresh toiletry kit. "If there's something we don't have, just call up to the house and Hazel will see that you get what you need. Hazel serves breakfast at six to the hands and at eight to the family. You're welcome to pick whichever suits you best."

Tucker stood somewhat dumbfounded. A mansion big enough for a hotel, a line of fancy and expensive cars in the driveway, and a stable with plenty of room for last-minute boarders. While none of that was a surprise unto itself, the generosity that seemed to come with it was a bit startling. Most ranchers he'd known had been decent folk—yeah, there were a few stingy, greedy S.O.B.s, but that wasn't the norm. A ranch couldn't function without its hands and ranchers tended to treat them well. But this layout for visiting hands was seriously over the top. Dollar signs were ringing over his head. Dollars he couldn't spare right now. "Don't mean to seem ungrateful, but how much do y'all charge for the night?"

The man who had quietly stood by as Tucker took in his surroundings seemed confused. "For what?"

"This." Tucker waved his arm across the room.

Something he said must have been funny, cause Mitch chuckled softly. "No charge. We've got the space, and you need it. Simple."

"Simple," he muttered softly. Not any kind of simple he'd ever run into. Still holding his hat in his hands, he turned to face Mitch. "I could be here a while."

The man nodded. "Understood."

"And you're not going to charge me?"

This time Mitch shook his head.

"Doesn't seem right."

"You *want* us to charge you?" The man wasn't quite smiling, but almost.

"Yeah, well."

Mitch said nothing, but his almost smile remained intact. Tucker had a feeling that the guy knew Tucker couldn't pay for it even if he wanted to.

"Does the ranch need any help?"

"A ranch always has more work to be done than time to do it."

Good. That's what he was hoping. "I have plenty of experience. I'd be happy to exchange an honest day's work for a night's stay."

"Seems like we'd be getting the better part of that deal. Hands receive free room and board *and* a paycheck."

He wasn't looking for a paycheck, but even he knew that the kind of care Thunder was getting wouldn't come cheap. After all, the pretty doc had bills to pay too. Maybe.

"Tell you what." Mitch's smile broadened. "Let's go take a look at how your horse has settled in and then we'll introduce you to Star. Then we'll see what kind of deal can be made. Sound good?"

Tucker nodded. Seemed fair enough.

The distance from the bunkhouse to the stable was much closer than the house to the stable. Again, no surprise there. Who wanted to smell a barn through their living room window? As they drew close to the barn, another person approached. In the dark Texas night, it wasn't until they were only feet apart that he recognized Devlin, the owner of the horse they were going to look at. He couldn't fathom learning to work with another horse in only a few weeks the way he worked with Thunder. At times, he felt as though that horse could read his mind. Why, the whole reason he got hurt was because he anticipated what Tucker was going to have to do. The horse just didn't take into account that when he changes direction and speed, and digs in deeper, he's more likely to injure himself.

"Thought I'd catch up with you here." Devlin nodded at them and handed him a cup. "Brought these from the kitchen. Star loves his apples."

"Thanks." He already had sugar cubes in his pockets. That was a happy treat for Thunder.

"Shall we?" Devlin waved his arm in the direction of the barn door.

Instead of following the hall straight ahead, they veered left and down and around to another area filled with stables. Just how big was this place?

"Star is down this way." Devlin smiled, his excitement at visiting the horse obvious.

With only those few words, a horse whinnied down the hall and if Tucker was correct, was tapping at his door.

Devlin's smile grew. "He's a good horse."

The moment Devlin opened the stall door, Star came up and nudged him in what was clearly an equine hug. Tucker stood back with Mitch, letting the two old friends visit a bit.

"I've got someone I want you to meet," Devlin spoke softly. "His name is Tucker. And he needs your help."

One ear twitched and Tucker knew the animal was carefully listening to every word.

Devlin waved Tucker in closer and took a step back.

The horse eyed him carefully. If Tucker thought he was here to size up the horse, apparently he had it backwards. Star was clearly sizing him up. Another moment and the horse nudged his side.

"You found it, huh?" Tucker pulled an apple half from the cup he'd stuffed in his jacket pocket and held it out. Star proceeded to happily chew down that and all the apple in the cup. When the horse was done, he looked at Devlin and nodded his head.

Devlin chuckled, stepped in to scratch behind the horse's ear, and looked to Tucker. "Seems you have his stamp of approval."

Everyone smiled, and for the first time since Thunder's injury, Tucker was actually feeling hopeful.

"If you're serious about wanting a little extra work," Mitch faced him, "we'll be working on the never-ending fence lines first thing in the morning. You're welcome to tag along."

"Will do." He nodded.

"All right then." Devlin stepped back. "I need to get back to town. I'll leave you two here."

"I'll walk with you." Mitch stepped up to his brother. "I've left Gwyneth alone long enough." He turned to Tucker. "You're welcome to stay and visit if you'd like, but we start before sunrise."

Tucker nodded and looked at the horse again. "You do have a light in your eyes," he told Star. "But if you don't mind, I have someone else I need to check on."

The horse actually nodded at him and nudged his other shoulder. The one that had the sugar in its breast pocket.

"So, you have a sweet tooth also." He gave the horse a cube and thought maybe he might even be shifting from hopeful to optimistic.

Turning the corner to the aisle that Thunder's stall was in, he slowly moved down, a soft voice growing a little louder.

"You're a sweet boy."

Coming to a stop at Thunder's door, he took in the scene. On the ground, Thunder laid back as Claire gently brushed his sides.

"Rest is good for you. Soon we'll have you up and running about. You're a good horse."

"He is." Tucker came into the stall and Thunder raised his head at the sound of Tucker's voice. "Stay, Thunder. Any man knows the touch of a good woman beats a visit with a buddy any day."

Her head immediately dipped closer to the horse, but for a second he was pretty sure he saw a tinge of pink paint her cheeks. So the lady embarrassed easily. Not what he expected from a vet who worked in what was mostly a man's world.

"No offense, ma'am."

"None taken." She continued to rub down the horse. "I

took a look at his X-rays. Nothing's broken or chipped, and the stitches look secure."

"Thank God."

Her head bobbed. "But he's still got a nasty cut. There's no way you can participate in the finals without making things worse."

"Agreed." He'd already known that without the X-ray. He squatted down beside her and scratched the ridge of Thunder's nose. "You do everything the nice doc tells you."

Not moving, Thunder moved his lips and Tucker took that for a yes.

"I'll be working with your brother, or cousin—someone—tomorrow on the fence lines."

"Great. It's good to stay busy."

"I'm also going to take Star through some simple paces. See how we work together."

"I hope it works out for you."

"Me too." He had a lot riding on the grand national finals. A whole lot.

CHAPTER FIVE

etting his alarm was not necessary. Normally, Tucker could sleep anywhere, on any surface. His friends even joked they could lean him against a wall and he could catch forty winks still standing. In this case, it wasn't the mattress, or the room, or location keeping him awake, it was all the things running through his head.

Nightmares taunted him. Visions of Thunder at the Nationals, falling, hurting himself because of Tucker's ambition. When that scenario faded, it was replaced with him on Star, and falling out of the saddle as the horse pranced into the arena and came to a sudden and stubborn stop. More images of him missing his last chance at a grand national purse and his own ranch, instead, sleeping in the backseat of his quad cab, a decrepit old man. One miserable scene after another. Except for one. The lady doc walking over to him after falling off the horse, and rather than tend to broken or bruised bones, leaned over and kissed him on the forehead and very softly whispered, *kiss the booboo all better.*

That last one had him shooting upright in bed, tangled in the single sheet, sweating like he'd been sleeping in a Swedish sauna. At four o'clock in the morning, he'd showered, shaved, and downed a cup of instant coffee. At nearly six in the morning, Mack, the foreman had rapped on the door announcing breakfast was served in the bunkhouse dining room. His belly full, and his brain slowly shaking loose of last night's dreams, he found himself teamed up with Mitch and another hand.

The Baron spread was one sweet operation. Everything ran so smoothly. Or maybe that was because he was working side by side with one of the owners. A note to self, if he ever got his own spread, never stop doing the hard work.

"Time for a break." Mitch led the way back to the pick-up, yanked a bottle of water out of the cooler and tossed one to the hand, then did the same to Tucker. The bigger surprise for Tucker was when he opened another cooler and pulled out a plastic tub. "Hazel made these last night. If you've got a sweet tooth, I recommend the jelly donut. If you'd rather have salty, there's cheese and crackers in the other tub."

Tucker didn't consider himself to necessarily have a sweet tooth, but he also couldn't see turning down fresh homemade donuts. "I think I'll take your recommendation."

The hand wasn't a fool either. Twenty minutes later, under the shade of a live oak that looked to be as old as Sam Houston himself, the three men had polished off the donuts, and two bottles of water.

"There's more water if you want." Mitch waved a thumb at the cooler.

"Any more and my back teeth'll be floatin'." The hand spat away from the wind and leaned back against the tree trunk.

"We'll be finishing up early here." Mitch took a last sip of his water bottle and tossed it into a nearby trash bag. "You thinking of working with Star?"

Tucker nodded. Despite his nightmares, he had a feeling about the horse.

"Devlin is very protective of that horse."

"Is he?"

"I suspect the only reason he agreed to this is he truly believes being in a competitive arena will make Star happy."

"Thunder isn't going to like being stuck in a stall for weeks."

Mitch tipped his hat back. "Would I be right in thinking that you feel the same way about Thunder as Devlin feels about Star?"

"Could be."

"Hazel seems to think the rodeo rose and set around you."

That had Tucker smiling. "Could be a bit of an exaggeration."

"A bit?" Mitch lifted a single brow.

Tucker shrugged. He wasn't one for bragging, or taking undue credit. "Thunder has a lot to do with that."

The Texas sun was growing strong and hot. Pulling a handkerchief from his pocket, Mitch rubbed his brow before straightening his hat. "With your help, we got further than I expected. I say we call it an early day. Then you can work Star in daylight."

He nodded.

"If you do as nicely in the arena as you do on a fence line, you should do well."

"That's the plan." One of the other things that had been bothering him last night and most of the day, why was everyone being so kind to him? "Does your sister make a habit of bringing home stray cowboys from rodeos?"

Mitch's brows rose even higher. "First off, Claire's my cousin, and secondly, she's an excellent veterinarian that will go above and beyond the call of duty if it's in an animal's best interest."

His mind wandered back to Claire crouched down by his horse, soothing him with a nice brushing. "I can see that."

"Perhaps what you should have asked me is if she's in the habit of bringing home stray animals. In that case, the answer is most definitely a resounding yes." Mitch pushed to his feet. "You are the first cowboy who has ever come home with an animal."

A silent moment settled over them before the other hand blinked and adjusting his hat to block the sun, stood and dusted off his jeans.

"If you're worried," Mitch grabbed the wire cutters he'd set down in the truck, "Thunder is in the best of hands."

The way Tucker saw it, he wouldn't mind putting himself in the pretty doc's hands. Then again, glancing at the way Mitch wrestled with a new post, minding his manners was in order. Such a shame.

"Atta girl." Claire called out to her newest nieces—well, almost nieces. They'd been coming to the ranch regularly for riding lessons, but it was Michelle the older girl who really took to the animals.

"She looks great, doesn't she?" Standing at her side, her sister Rachel leaned over the railing. "Has anyone discussed barrel racing for Michelle?"

Claire shrugged. "I honestly don't know. I haven't seen Leah for a few days, but you're right. Michelle sits a horse like she's done it for years."

"And look at that concentration. Her intensity on a horse reminds me of you."

As a teen, Claire loved barrel racing. She proudly displayed the ribbons she'd won all over her room. Every dresser top, every nightstand, stuck on posters, and anything else she could use. She loved all animals, but she lived and breathed for her horse.

"Look at that." Rachel whistled. "Perfect execution."

The kid had come a long way since the first time Claire saw her on horseback.

"Why don't you show her a few things?" Rachel pulled away from the railing. "As a matter of fact, I bet Mack would be willing to set up the arena so you can show Michelle what it looks like to be the best."

"Not the best anymore." The last time Claire got on a horse in an arena was for a charity rodeo her grandparents had sponsored three or four years ago. That was an awfully long time ago.

Rachel stuck a finger in each corner of her mouth and whistled loud enough to be heard in Oklahoma. Then she waved Mack, who had been working with Michelle more than anyone else, over.

"Yes, Miss Rachel?"

"How long would it take to set up the arena for a little

barrel racing display?"

"Rach," Claire actually whined.

The corners of Mack's mouth lifted in a smile so bright his eyes twinkled. "No time at all."

"See?" Rachel flashed a toothy grin and leaned forward. All Claire could do was shake her head.

"Something wrong?" A deep voice breezed past her.

"No," Claire answered Tucker, then turned to her sister, "and no."

"Come on," Rachel coaxed.

"Is there a problem?" Mitch came up behind Tucker and came to a stop next to Rachel.

"That's what I was asking."

Facing her cousin, Claire put one hand on her waist. "And I repeat. No." She spun about to face Rachel. "I am not barrel racing. Logan and Leah can take Michelle to a rodeo. Houston Rodeo is coming up soon. They'll have all the time in the world to see lots of horsemen."

"You're a barrel racer?" Tucker's words dripped with disbelief more than surprise.

Enough to raise her hackles. Holding her chin high, she leveled her gaze with his. "Something wrong with that?"

"No." He shook his head and actually took a step back. "I just wouldn't think a doc has time for racing."

"She doesn't." Mitch spoke up. "But I bet Michelle would get a kick out of it. I also bet she'll want to learn."

"And I know who can teach her," Rachel added, her grin wider than ever.

As her siblings spoke about her as if she weren't even there, Tucker seemed to be paying too much attention to the conversation. While she was busy arguing with her siblings and trying to ignore that Tucker was watching, Mack had wandered away and led Michelle into the stable.

"What do you think?" Rachel spun around and looked at Tucker. "Don't you think she should get on the horse and show her stuff?"

At Rachel's last words, Tucker's eyes briefly rounded and then settled back to normal. Had she noticed before what a deep color his eyes were? They reminded her of a crayon, only brighter.

"I, uh…" Tucker sighed. "Think that it's up to the doc."

While that wasn't a ringing endorsement, somehow it felt nice that he was sort of supporting her.

"If you don't think you can anymore…" Mitch let his words trail off and shrugged.

"Of course I still can race." Suddenly the need to prove her cousin wrong was stronger than her fear he might be right.

"Whatever you say." Mitch's agreement was cloaked in disbelief.

Blasted cousin. She took a step back and turned toward the stables. All the men in this family knew her buttons and Mitch had just pushed one. She's spent her whole adult life proving she was as good a big animal vet as any man, and as good a horsewoman. Of course she was going to get on a horse and risk breaking her neck. Walking several yards ahead, she shouted out to Mack, "Set 'em up. We're riding like the wind."

CHAPTER SIX

Tucker didn't know the doc very well, but he knew the instant she'd decided to ride the horse. She'd gone from *hell no* to *just watch me* in about five seconds. Something told him that her cousin pushing just the right button to get her to do what he wanted was not an uncommon thing. Banter like that had probably been going on for years, or even decades.

"You going to stick around for the show?" Mitch asked.

Tucker really wanted to. Very much. "I thought I would visit a bit with Star."

Mitch nodded. "Good idea."

"Mr. Mitch." The little girl that had been riding came running out of the stables. "Mr. Mack says that he has to do something for Miss Claire and I need someone to help me put up Misty."

"Sure thing." Mitch looked to Tucker. "If you'll excuse me, I have a horse to help tend to."

Tucker nodded. He was really starting to think more positively of politicians. The guy was sweet on his wife, respectful of his grandparents, not afraid to get his hands dirty, and considerate of small children.

Before he could say anything to Claire's sister, the woman had waved at him and taken off to where Mack was setting up barrels in the middle of the larger of two fenced in areas for exercising or training horses. Turning, he decided to stop first and check on Thunder.

As soon as he walked up to the stall, the horse had lifted his head. Even in unfamiliar territory, the animal recognized his walk. "How ya doing, fella?" Already Thunder was looking better. Where yesterday he was laying flat on his side, today he was sitting upright, like a sheepdog surveying his herd. Tucker sure hoped that meant the pain in his leg was easing.

From the other side of the stable, in the same area that Star was kept, he could hear a woman's voice. Slipping a sugar cube from his pocket, he held it out for his horse and tried not to pay attention to the voice.

"I shouldn't let them get to me," the voice spoke. "He might as well have said I dare you."

Even though he didn't want to eavesdrop, he still felt guilty hearing what she thought she was saying in private.

"How are those hooves looking? Has Mack been taking good care of you?"

He heard the horse nicker, and then she lowered her voice even more. The horse nickered again and Claire laughed. Tucker had no idea what the horse had done, but it was clear from what he could hear that she had a close relationship with the animal. He suspected from the way she treated Thunder and now dealt with this horse, she probably had a special way with every animal she came in contact with.

Scratching Thunder behind his ear with one hand, Tucker patted his horse with his other hand. "I need to go take care of some business, but I'll check on you again."

To his delight, Thunder bobbed his head in what Tucker chose to believe was an agreement that Tucker could go take care of his next task and that Thunder would be just fine. Though, Tucker had to admit, this was probably the biggest stall Thunder had ever been in. He suspected it was intended for birthing large animals, but then again, everything around Paradise Ridge seemed unusually nicer. Pushing to his feet, he made his way around the back hall to the other side of the massive stables and almost bumped into the backside of a horse.

To one side of the horse, Claire carried a large saddle.

"Here, let me help." Lunging forward, he reached for the saddle.

She twisted to one side. "I've got it."

"I'm sure you do, but that's no reason for me not to

offer to help."

Fire rose in her eyes. "If I need help, I'll ask for it."

And just like that, he realized he'd unintentionally done what her cousin had done, implied she wasn't capable. Quickly taking a step back, he held up his hands. "Sorry, ma'am. I'm going to see if it's okay with Mack for me to walk Star around in the smaller corral."

She nodded. "I'm sure that will be fine. Nothing rattles Star."

Tipping his hat to her, he walked over to where the foreman had come in from setting up for Claire's ride and secured permission. Next he found Star's stall and to his surprise, the horse almost seemed to be expecting him.

"I sure hope we're going to be friends."

The horse tipped his head to one side. Apparently, that was still on the table.

As he'd done with his own horse, he pulled a cube of sugar from his pocket and held his hand out to Star. "You might be my last hope."

It took the horse a second, maybe two, to make up his mind and gobble up the peace offering. Or bribe.

All of his plans for his future hung on this year's grand nationals. Winning the big purse would go a long way to securing that land he'd been coveting. "Shall we go for a walk?"

This time the horse did drop his head in an apparent nod. Tucker reached for a harness and lead, and slipping it on, led Star out of the stall.

Just as they crossed out of the stable into the open air, Claire walked past him with her horse. A beautiful chestnut. She paused to smile at him. "Good luck."

He bobbed his head. "Same to you."

"Right," she muttered as she paused and mounted the horse.

The next few moments took him by surprise. He'd just entered the smaller corral when he heard the sound of a whistle, like his gym teacher used to use to get the kids' attention, and from the other side of the large pen, Claire and her horse came flying.

He completely forgot what he and Star were doing. Both of them stopped, stone still, watching her aim for the first barrel and cut it so close he thought she was sure to knock the thing over, but nope. Precision, speed, and she was off to the next one. All he could think was, wow!

From the moment Claire guided her horse around the first barrel, both of them leaning into the turn, inches from the edge of control, adrenaline began fueling her ride. For a single moment, she feared riding too close the barrel might tip, but nope. She'd nailed the first turn. Every skill, every instinct she had, came to life as though the last time she'd done this had been only yesterday.

Any thoughts of Michelle, Tucker, or her family watching her performance faded into the background, the world narrowed to the thundering beat of hooves against dirt. With a surge of determination, she urged her horse onward, feeling the raw power coursing through her veins as they rounded the second barrel. One more barrel remained. Leaning forward, her ponytail bouncing in the wind, she and the horse racing forward as one, Claire felt the weight of time fall away, replaced by the exhilarating rush of freedom.

The third barrel only feet away, again she and her horse took the turn, dirt and dust kicking up behind them until finishing the turn, with all she had, she gently heeled her ride's flanks and raced out of the coral.

A small crowd had gathered along the side of the fence. Hats were waving in the air, whistles blew loudly, and voices echoed words of praise and cheer. The rush of excitement and pride took her back a decade or more. At a stop, she leaned forward on her mount, patted the horse's neck and whispered in one ear, "Atta girl. We did it again."

The horse swished its tail and bobbed its head.

Claire gave it one more pat. "I'll make sure you get a special treat tonight."

Again, the horse bobbed its head and with one hoof, pawed at the dirt. Definitely a happy horse.

"I'll take care of Pearl." Mack came up beside her and took the reins. "We'll give her an extra special rub down."

"Thanks, Mack. This girl deserves the royal treatment."

"Yes, miss."

"Can you teach me to do that?" Michelle held on to her dad's hand. Apparently, somewhere between her agreeing to this crazy display and finishing, Michelle's father had joined the crowd.

"That's up to your dad."

Blowing out a deep sigh, Logan nodded. "Even though it's against my better judgment, Leah persists in reminding me that you were a barrel race champion and are still alive to tell us about it. So, if that's what Michelle wants, then so it is."

Michelle spun around and hugged her father. "Thank you, Daddy."

"You're welcome, baby."

"Why don't you start something easy and show her how to handle a rope?"

Michelle turned to face her, the child's eyes wide with interest. "Like a cowboy?"

That had Claire chuckling. "Yeah." Before she could say yes or no or that cowgirls were as good as cowboys, despite what some of those cowboys believed, someone handed her a rope. Maneuvering it between her fingers, she spotted where someone else had set up the practice steer horns. Shaking her head, it looked like she was going to do one more display of skills long gone. Hopefully, she wouldn't make a total fool of herself in front of Michelle. Twirling the rope at her side, then over head, she let it fly. First try caught a horn. Yes! She repeated the effort three more times, three more captures. Perhaps, like riding a bike, you never forget.

"Can I learn that too, Daddy?"

Logan chuckled. "How about you learn that first and save your poor father's heart?"

The little girl bobbed her head with excitement and for

the first time in a long time, she wished so many men weren't jerks—or chauvinists. A few moments later, Logan and Michelle and a handful of other family members who had come out to watch, returned to the house.

It was going to take Claire hours to come down from the adrenaline rush. She still needed to check on Thunder, and now was as good a time as any. Partway to the barn door, she spotted Tucker walking and talking to Star. Like a magnet tugging her in, she shifted directions and walked over to the railing.

The moment Tucker spotted her resting against the rails, he turned to Star, rubbed under his jawline and, with his back to her, said something to the horse she couldn't hear. What she did know was that Star was listening to him. Loosening his hold on the lead, he and Star strolled over to where she stood.

"You were amazing." Tucker's head tipped toward the barn. "The horse wasn't bad either."

"The horse was magnificent. I think she loves the racing even more than I do."

"For what it's worth, I suspect you're right. What you two did out there was nothing short of magic."

"Many would say the same about you and Thunder."

He nodded. "They might, but that doesn't change the fact that you were magnificent to watch. Your roping skills are nothing to sneeze at either."

"Thank you." She glanced at the horse standing exceptionally close to him, considering they'd practically just met. "I see you two are bonding."

Tucker smiled. "I think we are."

"I hope this works out for you." She wasn't sure what else she could say, but for some reason, her feet didn't seem to want to move away. She liked talking to Tucker. Found herself wanting to know more about him.

"I checked in on Thunder. He's settling a bit better."

She nodded. "He is, but I'm afraid it will be a while before he feels well enough to stand more. Of course, he has to walk a bit every day. It's slow because of the leg, but he's a cooperative horse. Good spirited soul."

The sadness in his eyes showed how much Tucker cared for his horse. A good trait in a man as far as she was concerned.

"I was just going to check on him."

Tucker nodded, and slowly, sticking to her side, walked back into the stables. "Tell me, how many other stray horses have you brought home to care for?"

"Easy. One."

"That's it?" His brow rose on his forehead. "Your cousin made it sound like there was a parade of rescued animals coming through here."

"You didn't ask about all animals, you asked about horses." She couldn't help grinning up at him.

"Touché. Tell me about the horse."

"Story as old as time. I was on call at the rodeo when I heard a commotion. One idiot cowboy was unhappy with how his horse performed and he was whipping it as he screamed at him. There was no way I was going to stand for that. I stepped right up to him and told the jerk if he swung at that animal one more time I was going to swing at him."

"How did that go over?" A hint of sarcasm dripped from Tucker's words.

"Depends who you ask. He took a swing at me first, so I couldn't be blamed for breaking his nose. Enough people saw it for him to be arrested for assault and for me to load the horse and bring it here."

"You broke the guy's nose?" The incredulity in his voice might have bordered on admiration, even respect.

"I did. You don't grow up in a family with all these men and not learn how to defend yourself."

He nodded. Definitely respect. "Still have the horse?"

"Nope." She shook her head. "We gave him to friends of the family in West Texas. A horse breeder actually, but his cousin does equine therapy. I knew he'd have a good home with the Farradays. Turned out Shadow was cut out for that kind of work. Really gentle with kids and veterans."

"I've heard of the Farradays. One of them is a vet who sometimes fills in at the rodeos out that way. So tell me, what happened to the fist swinging cowboy?"

"Last I heard, our attorneys pretty much ran him out of state on a rail."

"Ever bring home any stray cowboys?" His tone didn't give even a hint of whether he was serious or teasing.

She tilted her head, leveled her gaze with his and smiled sweetly. "You're the first."

CHAPTER SEVEN

The days at the Baron ranch were flying by. Tucker found working with Star much easier than he'd expected. Having taken a few days to make friends with the animal had been the right move. Every day he was more hopeful that Star could be the answer to taking nationals. He and Mack, with Mitch's approval, had worked out a schedule where Tucker spent a few hours in the mornings helping out wherever help was needed, and his afternoons could be spent with Star. The only disappointing thing about this new arrangement was that not once had he bumped into Claire.

Grabbing a few treats from the tack room, he walked first to Thunder's stall. Today he'd arrived just as Mack was bringing his horse out of the stall. "I think he's not limping as much."

Mack smiled. "That's the idea. Always touchy to get a horse enough exercise to avoid complications, but not so much to set recovery back."

"Agreed." Tucker pulled a treat from his pocket and gave it to Thunder. "You're doing good, fella." He scratched at Thunder's jawline the way the horse liked and looked at Mack. "You want me to walk him?"

"Sure, if you want. All he gets though is to the doorway and back. And take it real slow. Like you're wearing high heels and the toes are pinching."

There was no way Tucker wanted to know how the heck Mack of all people had come up with that analogy or why the guy thought that walking in high heels would slow a man down. Not that Tucker knew any better.

The walk didn't take up much time. Just long enough

for Tucker to tell his horse how much he was enjoying working on the ranch. "You know, this is the kind of spread a man dreams of. Don't ya think?"

Thunder bobbed his head, nickered, then nudged Tucker's pocket for another treat.

Of course, that just made Tucker laugh. Handing the horse his treat, they turned around for the short walk back. "You really have it made, don't you? Fancy stall, people who care about you, and tasty treats. What more could a horse ask for?"

Despite the sore leg and limp, Tucker almost feared if the horse could talk, once he was recovered, he might argue to stay here instead of traveling from state to state and chasing steer. After returning Thunder comfortably to his stall, Tucker worked his way around to the other side where Star was. Doing the same as with Thunder, Tucker scratched the horse in his favorite spots, gave him some treats, and softly spoke to the animal about his day.

Once they were in the smaller of the corals, Tucker did as he'd been doing the last couple of days, just trotting and galloping around, gently nudging and directing Star with the slightest pressure of his legs or heel. Considering they hadn't been together long, the horse was crazy responsive. No wonder Devlin was so fond of the animal.

"Looking good." The familiar female voice sounded from the other side of the ring.

Spotting Claire stepping up to the railing, he waved. "Good horse."

Her booted foot resting on the lower rail, she set her arms along the top and leaned in to watch.

A little anxious at first over her watching, he scolded himself for reacting like a nervous schoolboy and focused on Star. Slowly, he went through the paces with the horse, so focused he almost forgot Claire was nearby—almost. When the fear of her leaving and him not getting a chance to visit at least a little grew strong enough to mess up his timing and concentration, he gave up and called it a day. Riding over to where Claire stood, he dismounted.

"Done for the day?"

"Yep. I really need to start working with roping. Your cousin tells me the ranch has all the training dummies I need for practice, but it's a bit late to set up today."

"Good. Then I can steal you away."

"Excuse me?" Why did those few words suddenly send sparks skittering down his spine?

Her head tipped up toward the house.

Instinctively, his gaze followed the direction she'd pointed. For the first time, he noticed the activity up at the house. "Looks like something brewing up there."

"Yep, the Governor loves any excuse to fire up the barbecue and summon the family."

"And what's the big event?"

"Danged if I know, but whoever is within driving distance will be here. If nothing else, there's always the promise of good food to go with the good fun. You want some help putting up Star before we head to the house?"

"No, I can…" her complete sentence suddenly registered, "we?"

She nodded. "I suspect there's a good chance that you're the guest of honor."

"The what?"

"You got straw in your ears?"

"Sorry. I guess I don't understand."

Claire shrugged. "Consider it southern hospitality."

The words 'at it's finest' came to mind, but he thought better of speaking them out loud. "I don't know."

She shrugged. "As I see it, you have two options. Put Star up and follow me to the house."

"Or?"

"Or, put Star up, head to the bunkhouse, and wait for the Governor to come drag you to the house."

A nervous chuckle erupted unexpectedly. Surprisingly, both prospects scared him silly, but one held way more appeal than the other. "I guess I'm following you then."

From the moment Claire had arrived at the ranch after a long morning at the clinic, she kept an eye out for Tucker. It had been days since they last crossed paths. She couldn't say why, but she'd looked forward to today's gathering, not so much for catching up with cousins she didn't get to see all the time, but for a chance to visit some more with Tucker. Most cowboys were nice people. Heaven knew chivalry came easily to all of them. Whether with polite greetings of ma'am, or tipping of a hat, or popping up to help with a heavy piece of equipment, they were all nice. But none had captured her interest the way Tucker had.

Maybe it was those dark blue eyes that seemed to have a near-hypnotic element if she stared into them too long. Or that sparingly shared crooked smile. Whatever, she'd already decided the guy was too nice to the horses to be a total jerk, and maybe getting to know him a little better wouldn't be the worst decision she'd ever made. The thought left her almost jittery with anticipation. When pretty much everyone had arrived, and still no sign of Tucker, she decided to go hunting.

As they grew closer to the house, Tucker's gaze scanned left to right, taking in all the people playing games on the lawn or chatting on the veranda. "How many people did the Governor invite?"

"Just family."

His eyes rounded wide with surprise. "How many cousins do you have?"

She couldn't help but laugh. "You don't want to know. Let's just say, a lot."

"A lot." Once again his head turned from one side to the other, silently bouncing from person to person, no doubt counting. "Are they all your siblings and cousins?"

"And their significant others."

"It's not a family, it's a small city."

That made her laugh even louder. "And this isn't even everyone."

The smell of smoked brisket wafted across the short distance to the veranda and Tucker's stomach growled. "Sorry. I might have skipped lunch."

"Don't tell Hazel, she'll overload your plate and insist on dessert too."

"Noted."

Shoving her hands in her pockets, she resisted an absurd urge to reach out and grab his hand. "This way to the food, but don't over eat, there will be S'mores after."

Their plates filled to the brim, he followed her down the hill to the first field where Adirondack chairs were scattered about and a handful of people were already settled in; eating, chatting and laughing. Claire led them to two chairs off to the side, close enough to be part of the fun, far enough away to have some semblance of privacy.

"Do y'all do this often?" He stabbed at some of Hazel's homemade cole slaw.

"Yes and no."

He shoved the forkful into his mouth and let out a deep low moan. "Wow. Who knew cole slaw could taste this good?" He stabbed at another forkful. "How can it be yes and no at the same time?"

Rib in hand, she shrugged. "Gatherings out here when the weather is pleasant is a common thing. Sometimes it's just food, sometimes there are games, sometimes there's a fundraiser, or a girl scout troop, or some other reason. Tonight, the Governor was in a mood for a bonfire and energized by having a couple of my cousins here who don't live close enough to come often."

He nodded. "Bonfire?"

Nodding, she swallowed and waved a hand down the slope. "There's a fire pit at the base of the field. As soon as dusk settles, someone will light it."

"As a kid, I loved making S'mores in the fireplace."

"Fireplace?"

He nodded. "My dad died when I was ten. We used to go camping every year, just the two of us. Mom wasn't a camper and was just as happy to stay home. The first year after Dad died, Mom tried so hard to make up for his loss. I probably wasn't the most agreeable kid."

"You were grieving."

"Yeah." He set his empty plate aside. "One evening

after dinner, she turned on a couple of oil lanterns, turned off the lights, and lit the fireplace." That slow smile that she found so appealing tugged at one corner of his lips. "I thought she was losing her marbles, but she came out with a tray of fixings for S'mores. We talked, really talked, for the first time. It wasn't the same as camping with Dad, but it was a sweet time. Mom and I did living room camping one weekend every summer till I graduated high school."

Images of a little boy missing his dad flashed before her and her heart melted just a little bit. Then her mind shifted to what her brothers were doing in their teens. Hanging out with their mom or dad was not coming to mind. "You hung out with your mom even when you were a teen?"

He nodded. "Not cool I know, but that weekend was important to me. Once a year, Mom stopped being the parent and was just my friend. It was fun." His smile lifted higher. "I learned a lot about life, dating, and…stuff from her on those weekends. And for the most part, she was right."

"Only the most part?"

Still smiling, he shrugged. "Maybe always."

Having finished her food, she pushed to her feet. "Come on, let's get good seats."

On his feet, he fell into step beside her. When she tripped over a divot in the ground and pitched forward, he reached out and grabbed her, steadying her in front of him. "Careful. You okay?"

Her hands settled on his chest, her eyes leveled with his, and she wasn't at all sure if he let go of her if her legs would hold up. "I, uh, guess I tripped."

Carefully, he eased his grip on her, but didn't quite let go.

For just a moment, she wondered if he didn't want to let go as much as she wished he didn't have to. "We should keep, uh, going." With more regret than she'd expected, she stepped back and away from his touch.

At the bottom of the hill, Tucker started chuckling.

"What's so funny?"

"When you said bonfire, you weren't kidding." The real

wood fire pit was larger than most to accommodate a crowd the size of the Barons.

"If the plan weren't to toast S'mores but just to enjoy the burn, that thing would be as tall as I am."

"Don't suppose you have any Aggie engineers in the family," he teased.

"As a matter of fact." Smiling, she rocked on her toes. "Two. Three if you count my cousin Kyle's wife."

"That explains a lot."

"I beg your pardon?" She dared to move in closer. When Tucker's eyes met hers and dark blue seemed to be reading her soul, she almost lost her breath. How could she react so strongly to a man she barely knew?

"I, uh," his gaze remained fixed with hers, "wonder if, since tomorrow is Saturday and all, if maybe, you might… be willing to join me for dinner"?

Her head bobbed, but her mouth didn't move.

Tucker snapped his fingers. "Darn it. I forgot that I wanted to check out a rodeo just north of here. See what my competition's doing." He sucked in a long breath. "I don't suppose there's any chance you'd have time to come with me?"

Even if she had to move every appointment under the sun and arm wrestle every man in her family, she would not miss out on a day with Tucker and the chance to figure out what it was about him that made him almost irresistible. No matter how hard she tried not to think of him, the more she got to know Tucker Pride, the more he seemed to work his way into her thoughts. Finally, finding her voice, she muttered, "Yes."

CHAPTER EIGHT

nyone would think Tucker had never been out with a woman before. He actually changed his shirt three times. Thank heavens jeans were the only option for pants or he might have changed those several times as well. If he weren't positive that every experienced rodeo man would laugh him out of the arena, he would have polished his boots. Next time he invited Claire out to dinner there wasn't going to be a rodeo with dusty boots involved.

Pausing for a second, he realized he really wanted a next time. Very much. Not that it made any sense. Claire was very pretty, but he'd known a lot of pretty women. She was also smart, but that wasn't exactly an anomaly either, and she certainly wasn't the only animal lover on the planet. Yet, combine all of the above and that heart-stopping smile, and he was completely and totally smitten. Too bad he hadn't had time for a haircut. Hopefully, she liked the carefree, slightly overgrown look.

Stepping out of the guest bunkhouse, he crossed over to where his truck was parked and frowned. Turning on his heel, he marched back inside, grabbed a roll of paper towels, filled a spray bottle with water and marched more heavily back to the truck. It took at least ten minutes, maybe fifteen, but now his truck no longer looked like a construction worker's catch all and was more suitable for transporting a lady. Driving around to the front of the main house, he sat behind the wheel for a moment longer than necessary. The house was impressive in stature and care. Meticulously pruned landscaping filled with multi-color blooms and perfectly trimmed shrubs greeted every guest and family member alike. Despite the obvious wealth behind the massive walls, the home shouted welcome.

In all of his dreams, his imagination couldn't conjure up anything quite like this. Everything here, everything about the Barons, was so far removed from the doublewide he'd grown up in. What was he even doing here? Who was he kidding? Claire Baron may be the only woman to fully capture his attention since his sixth grade algebra teacher broke his leg and the school saw fit to provide a pretty substitute teacher with long legs and curves that put an hour glass to shame, but just like Miss Sweeney, Claire was out of his league.

"Keep it business," he muttered to himself. That was the sensible thing to do. Pushing the vehicle door open, he hopped out of the truck and took the front steps two at a time. Already his heart was beating double time, not from the stairs, but anticipation of seeing Claire. "Business," he reminded himself.

After ringing the doorbell, he kept silently repeating those words to himself until the door swung open and a smiling Claire stood on the other side bouncing on one foot.

"Come on in. I have to run upstairs real quick and change my shoes." Holding a boot in her hand, she waved him in. "Brand new and the stupid heel came off when I tripped over the dog."

"How's the dog?" He smiled and followed her inside.

"Perfectly fine. I'd suggest you go inside and visit with Grams and the Governor, but then we'll never get out of here."

"Here you go, Miss." A woman in an apron came running down the stairs holding a boot in each hand. "I picked your favorite pair."

"Thanks, Margaret." Flopping onto the bottom step, she made quick work of putting on the old boots and then jumped to her feet. "Ready if you are."

That he wasn't sure of, but he held the front door open for her, and then the same with his truck door. "I'm afraid I didn't have time to clean it up, but I did neaten it up a bit."

She shrugged. "You don't want to see what a mess my truck is. This is luxury."

He almost spit with laughter. By now he knew exactly how much luxury these people lived in and not by any stretch of the imagination would anyone use that word to describe his beat-up old truck.

For the first few minutes, as he drove off the property and down the narrow winding roads, they rode in silence. Once he had their destination plugged into his phone, the voice immediately announced his next turn and he tried not to cringe.

Across from him, Claire chuckled softly.

At least she wasn't frowning. "Sorry. On long drives she keeps me from falling asleep."

"I bet." She chuckled a little louder.

"Five hundred feet, turn right, big boy," the sultry voice directed.

"Maybe I should pull over. You know, change the voice to that computerized monotone."

"Nah." She shook her head and waved at him. "Mine is British."

"What?"

"My GPS. I picked the British voice. If I could get specific I would have picked Daniel Craig, but we all need to keep awake when driving a lot."

She got it. And apparently wasn't holding it against him. So, he could add a sense of humor to her other positive qualities. This strictly business plan of his was going to be even harder than he thought.

There was no way Claire was telling Tucker that until recently, her GPS voice had been the hard-boiled noir detective. Even though she felt sorry for the poor guy. The first moment the sultry female voice breathed her directions, Claire could see the hint of red creeping up his neck. The guy was absolutely adorable when he blushed. She'd have to add that to the list of things she found irresistible about Tucker Pride. Right about now a good change of subject was in order. "Were you supposed to compete in today's rodeo?"

He bobbed his head. "Shouldn't matter, though. Unless something absurd happens, I should have enough points to still make it to the grand national finals."

His embarrassment gone, she noticed a tight set to his jaw. "I detect a 'but' lingering there somewhere." Angling to better see him, what she couldn't figure out is why did he look so serious. "You don't think Star can cut it?"

"Star is a great horse. He catches on quick to my maneuvers, but it took Thunder and me a good long time until he could read my mind, or even better, anticipate the next move before I could."

"Good horse."

"Very good. I know this sounds silly…" That blush began creeping again. "I feel like I'm cheating on Thunder or something. Considering another horse."

Okay, so the guy is adorable and loyal. The positive checks were growing. "I can see that. It's always hard to step back from a good team."

For the rest of the ride, the conversation was all over the place, from horses, to Texas, to the antelope in Wyoming outnumbering the people, to sports, and of course, family. Hers was insanely huge, and ridiculously close, and she wouldn't have it any other way.

They pulled into the parking lot and before she could unbuckle, Tucker was opening her door. "Thanks."

He bobbed his head. "My pleasure. Appreciate the company. Hopefully, it will stop me from overthinking this."

"I'll do my best."

Walking side by side, she breathed in the familiar scents of the rodeo. Normally, when she was the doc on call, there was a different mindset, no time to appreciate the energy and aromas all their own. From the leather, the horses, the hay, the sweat and the must-have barbecue, she loved every one of them. Well, maybe not the sweat so much.

"Hey, Tuck." A tall lanky cowboy in a red shirt frowned. "You riding today?"

"Nope. Just here for the show."

The man's face relaxed and a hint of a smile appeared. "We'll do our best to put on a good one for you."

Tucker chuckled and slapped the other guy on the shoulder. "You do that."

"Oh," the man hesitated, "and by the way, really sorry to hear about Thunder. How's he doing?"

"Good. Better every day."

The man nodded and tipped his hat at Claire. "See y'all later, maybe."

"I gather you know him well," Claire said when the man walked away.

"I do. He won the grand final last year."

"Ah." She fell into step beside him as they moved down the way.

"Something to drink?" He stopped by the wall of vendors.

"Light beer."

"A beer?"

"Don't look so surprised."

"Sorry." He smiled and turned ordering two beers then moving over to the next booth. "Do you like nachos?"

"You're kidding? That's a sacred food group in Texas. Although it's hard to compare with the white queso at an Austin restaurant."

"Austin. Kirby's?" His head tipped.

"That's the one. Best queso in the world."

"Might have to agree with you." He bobbed his head and ordered two nachos.

She leaned into the counter and looked at the clerk. "Add jalapenos to mine, please."

"Oh, you are a woman of many surprises."

"That chauvinist is raising his head again."

He turned to the kid behind the counter. "Make them both with jalapenos." Then he turned to face her. "Why does being surprised make me a chauvinist?"

"If my brother asked for jalapeno on his nachos, would you have been surprised?"

Chuckling, he tipped his hat back and scratched the side

of his neck. "Okay, maybe, just maybe, I would not have been surprised, but not because I'm a chauvinist, just because…" he seemed to be at a loss for words.

And she burst out laughing. "You may want to quit before you dig yourself deeper into a hole."

He blew out a sigh. "For now. I may want to keep silent until I can have my one phone call."

It took her a moment to connect the dots of one phone call to your lawyer before she chuckled again and reached for the nachos the clerk had slid in front of them. Beer in one hand and nachos in the other, she looked ahead. "Where to now?"

"Our seats."

She followed him down the walkway and up the steps into the bleachers. Settled in, she was still munching on her nachos when the bare-back riding event started. Watching Tucker was more interesting than watching the riders. His facial expressions ran the gamut from blank, to tense, to head nods and deep sighs. The guy in the red shirt came out and Tucker remained stone faced. Next came the barrel racers. The first woman who came riding in, she kept her gaze on Tucker, the second rider, Claire was on the edge of her seat. She recognized the name and the face from church. The subject of barrel racing had never come up.

"You miss it?" His gaze was fixed on her.

"If you'd asked me a few weeks ago, I would have honestly said no."

"But today?"

"Today." She tipped her head to meet his gaze. "Yeah. A little."

"You know," his gaze drifted to the woman circling the third barrel and racing out of the arena then back to Claire, "there are lots of amateur rodeos you could do from time to time just for fun."

"Yes, but between work and family, I don't really have time for it." She blew out a sigh. "I did that for a little while, but unlike city vets with set office hours, a large animal vet in ranch country can get pulled away any time of day, seven days a week."

His smile widened, ignoring the next racer thundering around the arena. "And you love that too."

It wasn't really a question, but she nodded anyhow. "More than barrel racing, but…" She watched the last woman in the schedule shoot into the arena and bang into the second barrel before hurrying on. "It would be nice, I mean, once in a while."

His gaze turned to the first team flying into the arena in the roping event. "Yeah, once in a while."

To her, it didn't sound like his comment was about her wants, or even about the action unfolding in front of them. Noticing his nachos were empty, she extended the last few in her paper dish. "Want one?"

Looking at her for longer than she would have expected, he reached out, picked out a nacho, and as he pulled back, his hand brushed lightly against hers. The unexpected heat caught her by surprise. He must have felt it as well because he'd just as suddenly lost interest in the happenings in the arena. When his gaze dropped for just a second to her lips, she knew he'd felt what she had. The question at hand now was, what the heck was she going to do about that?

CHAPTER NINE

"**S**o." Claire swung her purse over her shoulder and pushed to her feet. The last event had ended, the guy in the red shirt took the biggest prize for the night, and Tucker's brows had remained knit together for the last hour. "Barbecue?"

Tucker shook his head. "Real dinner."

"As opposed to a fake dinner?"

He held out his hand for her to take as they climbed down the stairs to the main level and abruptly let go as they hit the bottom landing. "I invited you to a dinner out, not a rodeo barbecue."

Regretting the loss of his touch, she forced a smile. "Have some place in mind?"

"Do you have a favorite food?"

"Italian." She shrugged. "I'm a sucker for a good marinara sauce."

"Then I know exactly where we're going." His hand landed gently on the small of her back as he helped maneuver her through the throngs of people leaving the arena or heading to the cafeteria-like restaurant set up with the barbecue.

Once again, as they exited the arena, he took back his hand and she wondered when was the last time she'd been out with a man who rather than avoid their advances, she wished he'd make one.

In the parking lot, he opened the truck door for her, then once she was settled inside, hurried around to the driver side. "I hope you like Mom and Pop joints."

"Usually the best food."

"You got that right." Pulling out of the parking lot, he

came to a stop at the light and turned to face her. "I found the place several years ago after the rodeo here. Since I was in town for several days, I kept going back. Did the same thing every time I was in town."

"Now I'm really looking forward to it." She settled in as the truck continued down the road. "Would I be correct in guessing you like Italian food too?"

"Love it. My grandmother learned to make red sauce from her Italian grandmother. My mother didn't like cooking so she never really learned how. Nonna died when I was a thirteen. Too young to realize I should have asked her to teach me."

"You like to cook?"

"Don't look so surprised. I have no interest in going to cooking school or anything, but I can fend for myself in the kitchen."

Loosening the seat belt, she shifted to face him. "What's your best meal?"

"Toss-up between my meatloaf or coca cola pot roast. Though I've been told mac and cheese is my best dish."

"Okay, I'm sorry, but that is way more than fend for yourself. Unless your mac and cheese comes in a box."

He laughed and turned the corner. "No box. The secret is adding a little Gouda and topping it with Ritz crackers instead of ordinary bread crumbs."

"Really? The Gouda sounds great, but I can't decide if the crackers are better or worse than bread crumbs."

"Only one way to find out. I'll have to make it for you some day."

"Deal."

One more corner and he pulled into a small strip center. In the far corner, a lit-up sign announced they'd arrived at the Amore Café. Outside, a few café tables adorned either side of the glass door. Inside, the tables were covered with red and white checkered tablecloths. Rather than the expected small flower vase that usually decorated tables, Chianti bottles coated with colorful wax drippings held a single burning candle.

This was by far the quaintest Italian restaurant she'd

ever been in this side of the Atlantic. Instantly she was taken back to a small village near Lake Como and the best little Italian restaurant she'd ever eaten in. Something told her she was in for a treat tonight.

"Tucker. Mi amore." An older woman who was almost as wide as she was tall came up to him sporting a huge smile. No surprise when she squeezed his cheek before kissing both of them. "I was hoping you'd come visit Mama."

"Mama Antoinette, this is my friend Claire."

The woman's smile actually grew wider. "Ah. You bring me a girl." Her gaze briefly went from head to toe and back. "A nice girl too." Her brow pleated. "It's about time you find a nice girl. Come sit. I'll bring you your favorite calamari marinara."

"I love calamari marinara," Claire said.

"See?" Mama waved a finger at him. "I knew it. A nice girl."

They both followed the happy woman, and Tucker leaned into her, his voice just below a whisper. "Sorry about that."

"I think it's charming. I feel like I'm in Italy. Although calamari marinara reminds me of New York. I've never found a restaurant in Texas that doesn't fry their calamari."

Tucker pulled out her seat for her and Mama stood with her arms folded, grinning like a woman admiring a master's painting. "See, he's a nice boy. Yes?"

Her gaze darting quickly to Tucker and back, she dipped her chin. "Very nice."

"My Carina will be here in a minute to take your order." Without another word, the woman turned on her heel and hurried into the kitchen.

"How often did you say you came here?" She draped her napkin across her lap.

He shrugged. "A few days every year."

"And she remembers you like that?" Of all people, she knew how captivating Tucker could be, but that was a lot of love for a restaurant owner he saw only a few days a year.

His eyes lowered to the table, and he turned his fork

between two fingers.

"Something wrong?" She didn't like the cloud that seemed to fill his eyes.

"No." He blew out a sigh. "About three years ago, I was the last one to leave after another delicious meal here. When I got to my truck, my phone rang. Instead of driving off, I stayed in my truck to talk. I don't know how long I'd been there when I saw Carina come out the door and lock it behind her. To this day, I don't know why I watched her walk to her car."

She couldn't help but smile.

He stopped speaking and tilted his head. "Why are you smiling?"

"I know why you watched her." She shrugged.

"Why?"

"You're a gentleman."

"I thought I was a chauvinist?" Now he was smiling again.

"Maybe that too." She chuckled and was sure she was blushing. "I'm sorry, continue the story."

His smile immediately slipped away. "She was unlocking the car when a tall figure came out of the shadows. Carina backed up and I knew from her stance it wasn't good."

Instinctively, Claire's hand rose to her chest and her heart picked up. Just like a dark film, she was afraid to hear what came next.

"Needless to say, I'd never flown out of my truck so fast in my life. To make a long story short, one broken arm later and as far as I know, the perv's still behind bars."

"You saved her." It wasn't a question.

"That's what Mama says. I did what any person would have done."

Unfortunately, the world was full of people who either didn't pay attention or didn't want to get involved. Even if he didn't want to admit it, she knew the same thing Mama knew, Tucker wasn't like the jerks that had come and gone in her life, he was a good man. A very good, old-fashioned, caring man.

Telling what happened that night almost felt like a betrayal of Carina's privacy. Somehow he knew that a generic throw away response wouldn't have satisfied Claire. She was smart as well as intuitive. Still, there was no need to point out that in the brief time it took him to cross the parking lot, the asshat had sliced Carina's blouse open, cut her arm, and threatened to do the same to her face. By the time he reached her, adrenaline and fury rushed so hard and fast in his veins, if a passing police car hadn't noticed him pummeling the assailant, Tucker honestly thought he could have killed the man.

"On the house." Petite with long dark hair pulled back in a ponytail, Carina came up to the table and set a plate of stuffed mushrooms on the table. "From Mama. Your favorite."

"Thank you." Tucker smiled up at her. No matter how much time passed, he still thought of Carina as a sweet kid. Having graduated college did nothing to make her look more grown up in his eyes.

"I love stuffed mushrooms." Claire stabbed at one with a fork and set it on her plate. Slowly, using her fork and knife, she sliced it in half and then took a bite. "Oh, my. This is delicious."

It gave him immense pleasure to see her enjoy the food so much. "I have tried to schmooze Mama into sharing the recipe, but the woman has willpower of steel."

"If this is our starter, I can hardly wait to see what the rest of the meal will taste like."

As he expected, Claire ordered the calamari marinara. She added a side of angel hair pasta and he ordered the same with an order of cheesy garlic bread.

When Carina brought their meal, Claire dug into the calamari much like a child would dig into an ice cream sundae. The look of sheer delight on her face made him smile. When her eyes closed and she moaned with delight, he shifted in his seat and battled thoughts he had no business thinking.

"This is the best calamari I've ever had. Even better than New York." She chewed for another moment and her gaze narrowed. "The calamari is fresh?"

He bobbed his head. "They buy them fresh off the shrimp boats. It's not uncommon for the squid to get caught in the nets."

Her nose crinkled and she waved a fork at him. "Squid sounds so much less appetizing. I'll stick to calamari."

That made him laugh. "So what you're saying is that a rose by any other name may not be a rose."

She set her fork down and chuckled with him. "Something like that."

The two of them continued to chat about everything and anything that came to mind. He discovered that she was a huge football fan and had learned to like hockey when her cousin married a former hockey star. They discussed the last Superbowl and it hadn't surprised him in the least to learn they'd rooted for the same team. There was a lot about Claire that fell into step with his likes and interests. None of which he would have expected from someone with as much money and social standing as her. Then again, after meeting so many in her family, he clearly had the wrong idea about the ultra-rich. Or at least, one ultra-rich.

"Can we interest you in dessert?" Carina stood over the table smiling sweetly. It had taken a few returning visits before she finally lost the skittishness that had cloaked her after the parking lot incident. It took a while longer for those smiles to reach her eyes. Today in particular, there seemed to be an extra sparkle in her gaze.

"I'll have my usual." He turned to Claire. "Italian crème cake for me, please."

"Two Italian crème cakes coming up." Carina took a step back and Tucker reached for her hand, slowing her steps.

"You seem especially happy tonight. Care to share?"

Her smile bloomed and her cheeks pinkened.

"Go ahead. Tell him," her mother called from the kitchen. He'd forgotten Mama had hearing that could put the bionic woman to shame.

"Mama," she practically whined, rolling her eyes skyward.

"Good news?" he asked.

Carina grinned again. "I'm sort of engaged."

"Sort of?" He looked to Claire to see if he'd missed something, but her face held the same confusion he felt.

"You remember the guy I was dating?"

It took him a minute to remember the young man who never took his eyes off of her. "I do."

"We went to a dinner and a show the other night to celebrate his graduating with his masters."

Tucker bobbed his head. Nice. He liked that. Even if he was allergic to school books.

"He got down on one knee and everything." She rubbed her ring-less finger. "My Uncle Vincenzo is a jeweler. We're going to pick out a ring next weekend. He didn't want to pick something out that I wouldn't like."

"Very thoughtful," Claire spoke up. "He sounds like a nice man."

"He is." Carina's smile was so wide and her eyes so happy, her joy was contagious.

"Congratulations." Tucker squeezed her hand. "And you tell Kenny if he even thinks of stepping out of line, he'll have me to deal with."

"Don't you worry," Mama once again hollered from the kitchen. "I already told him for you."

Both he and Claire bit back a chuckle.

Carina rolled her eyes and softly mumbled, *Mama.* "I'll get your desserts."

Once she was out of ear shot, Claire leaned forward and took hold of his hand. "Have you met him? Is he really a nice guy?"

Resisting the urge to look down at her hand on his, he nodded. "Didn't say much the few times I saw him here waiting for Carina to get off work, but any idiot could tell he was way more than smitten. The man's gaze never left her. Reminded me a bit of a lost puppy. A six-foot-tall lost puppy."

That made Claire chuckle. Lifting her hand away from his, she leaned back. "I'm glad. I like her."

The cake arrived and he paused just a moment to consider, once again they'd chosen the same item. Had the same taste. Only difference was that he wished she hadn't let go of his hand. He very much wanted to reach out and snatch her hand in his. If he were honest, he'd been wanting to do that all night. Now he asked himself, if he tried to hold her hand on the way to the car, would that be the start of something wonderful, or the end of what wasn't meant to be?

CHAPTER TEN

Sunshine crept into Claire's room. Opening one eye, she glanced at the clock on her nightstand. Too early, but she was awake, and her grandparents were expecting her for dinner tonight, which to her grandmother meant arriving before lunch. Rolling over, she grabbed the extra pillow and curled into it. A few more minutes of daydreaming wouldn't make her too late.

The rodeo and dinner last night had been so much fun. More than once she'd had to resist the urge to hold Tucker's hand and not let go. Every time he gently placed his hand at her lower back, she felt the loss when he moved away. She could not remember the last time she had wanted so badly for a man to kiss her. Once or twice, she actually debated kissing him. Only the fear of how awkward that would be until he and Thunder moved on kept her from doing anything foolish.

Her mind had wandered off to moments last night. When she reached over and momentarily covered his hand with hers. When his hand settled on her back as they walked away from the table. The way he stood holding the car door open, not quite close enough to kiss, but she second-guessed herself. What would he have done if she'd leaned forward and stood on tippy toes to kiss him? Shaking her head, she pushed herself upright. She was behaving like a besotted teen. She was a grown woman and daydreaming about handsome cowboys was absurd.

Throwing her feet over the side of the bed, she blinked, stretched and stood just as her phone beeped. Looking down, the number brought a smile to her face. It took her a moment to actually look at the message. For just a minute, she enjoyed the contentment that seeing Tucker's name appear on her phone gave her. Still smiling, she tapped on the phone.

Thank you for dinner.

Her cheeks tugged at the corners of her mouth. A small part of her was afraid the text was an issue with the horse, but no, the message was personal. That made her even happier than seeing his name. Such a teenage reaction.

Thank you. She wanted to say more but didn't want to say too much.

I had a really nice time.

At first she typed *me too*, then erased it and thought about it a moment. There really wasn't much else she could say. *So did I. Everything was perfect. The restaurant, the food.* She sucked in a deep breath. Here went nothing. *And the company.* Waiting for his response, she was almost holding her breath, about to curse herself for saying too much when the phone dinged in her hands.

Awesome company.

"Yes!" Phone in one hand, she did a fist pump with the other and threw in a small jig to go with it.

Another dinner?

Another invitation. That was good. Especially if she could figure out how to get a little hand-holding in and maybe even a kiss. *That would be nice.*

Tonight?

Except tonight. Okay. Think. How ticked off would her grandparents and siblings be if she missed family dinner for a date. Looking at the phone, she actually asked herself one minute if it could be considered a real date and the next minute she was chastising herself—of course it was a date. And she knew that several of her cousins were going to be at dinner. If they found out she skipped for a date, she'd be teased by half and her grandfather would have her marching down the aisle. *I can't tonight. Family dinner.*

Oh. Of course

Join me? It took her a moment to realize what she'd done. If going out on a date was like dangling a carrot in front of a race horse, bringing the date to dinner was like the starter gun going off at a race.

At the ranch? With your grandparents?

Yes. Just for the heck of it she added a smiley face. Somebody should think it's a good idea.

Silence hung and she figured he was probably worrying about the same things she was. Or maybe he was concerned that she was making more of this than he intended. More of this. Oh for the love of horses, what was she thinking inviting him to dinner with the family. Of course he was hesitant. Even though he'd met the family already, that was as a visiting horseman; this was, well, her guest.

She let her head fall against her open palm. How was she going to gracefully get out of this? She was still typing *no worries, rain check* when her phone dinged again.

Sounds nice. What time?

Surprise washed over followed a moment later by giggles and the need to do another jig. *I'll be there in a couple of hours.* No need to mention she needed lots of coffee first. *Need to check on Thunder. Will let you know when I'm there.*

Okay, came back, immediately followed by a smiley face.

She debated responding but decided that she needed to play it at least a little cool. This was so out of her realm. Normally she and her siblings and cousins had to be wary about a person's interest. If not wary, at least guarded. Being too forward or pushy wasn't the norm, but danged if she didn't want to push.

Out of bed and making her morning coffee, her mind was still dancing around the invitation to dinner. Visions of her brothers grilling Tucker popped uninvited into her head. Her grandparents always served a somewhat formal dinner. She should probably warn him. Later, in person. Pouring the coffee, now her mind jumped to would he mind? Would he be thrown off by all the forks and flatware? Would he notice that the silverware was really silver? Swallowing her first long slow sip, she cradled the mug in both hands and worried if she'd just screwed up her chances with the nicest cowboy she'd ever wanted to know better.

Training with Star as a distraction from thoughts of Claire was not working at all. When Star nudged him, Tucker realized, he wasn't fooling anyone, not even the horse. "I'm sorry, boy." He stopped in place and turned to face his newest friend. "There's something about her that is just… different."

To his surprise, the horse nodded and nudged him again.

"I know. I'm trying. I don't want to rush her."

Star lifted his head, moved his lips and bumped Tucker's hat.

"I gather you don't agree."

The horse actually shook his head and this time succeeded in knocking Tucker's hat off.

Bending over, he retrieved his hat, whacked it against his thigh and rather than return it to the top of his head, held on to it. "I'm joining her for dinner, but that's as fast as I'm going, no matter what you think."

If it were possible for a horse to roll his eyes, Star probably would have.

"Let's get you back to your stall." Tucker scratched the horse's jaw just as his phone dinged with a new message. His heart jumped at Claire's name, and he tapped the screen.

I'm pulling into the driveway. Meet me at the house?

Star nudged him again.

"Yes. It's her. And I have to go." Anxious to meet up with Claire, he asked Mack to take care of Star and get him back to the stall. Leaving the barn, he resisted the urge to run to the house. Knowing how long the drive onto the property was, he opted to rush up to the front of the house instead of the back in an effort to head her off.

At the top of the hill, he turned the corner onto the lawn just as her car pulled up by the front steps. Not wanting to look too eager, he sauntered over and came to a stop as she circled the hood of her car.

"Hi." Her grin was infectious.

"Hey." He waved and then shoved his hands into his pockets rather than reach for her.

"Have you seen anyone?" She slung her purse over her shoulder.

He shook his head. "Been working with Star."

"Oh." Her smile brightened. "How's that going?"

"Actually, much better than I thought." He wasn't going to mention the horse was a tad bossy and opinionated. She would think he'd lost his mind.

"Wonderful." She pushed the front door open and dropping her purse on a nearby table, hurried to the back of the large foyer.

Even though he'd been inside the home briefly when he'd picked Claire up the other night, walking into the foyer still took him aback. The other night he'd been more aware of Claire, how cute she looked hopping on one foot and how much he was looking forward to going out with her. Tonight, he was much more aware of his surroundings. With every step, he felt as though he were walking through a magazine spread. Each piece of furniture managed to scream high class and welcome at the same time.

When they crossed into what he assumed was the family room, he was struck once again by the enormity of the space, and yet, the cozy feel of it all. High ceilings that could have made the room feel cavernous, instead the coffered ceilings with soft wood tones brought warmth to the space. Right along with the hum of conversation. He knew Claire came from a large, close family. After all, he'd already met quite a few of them. Still, the number of people mulling about would have been more stifling in a normal sized living room.

"Lovely to have you join us this evening." Lila Baron looked up from her spot in a comfy chair. A dog sat at her side, tail swishing in rhythm with its gaze taking in the room, and the new visitor.

Taking in a deep breath, he reminded himself that no matter how much money these folks had, they still put their boots on one foot at time like anyone else. "Thank you for having me."

"Mack tells me that you're getting along well with Devlin's horse." The Governor, who had been reading an actual newspaper, set it down on his lap.

"I believe we are."

"You thinking of doing anything with him?" Claire's brother Cooper stood by a bar pouring drinks.

"I'm thinking about it." He was actually past the point of considering if and had moved on to could they do it. Could they win?

A bustle of noise carried from the foyer as a cluster of people came through the doorway. Tucker recognized Mitch and his wife, he had no idea who the other person following them inside was, but the way all the folks in the living room stopped what they were doing and jumped to their feet, rushing over to the baby that Mitch held, he was fully aware of who the star of the day was going to be.

Even the men were waving fingers and making faces at the young infant, but Claire was the first to snatch the baby from her father's arms.

"Hey there, my little one." Claire's voice was soft and low and reminded him of the way he'd overheard her talking to Thunder. "We are going to have so much fun when you're old enough to have sleepovers and go shopping…"

She was still planning out the kid's future with her sister Rachel at one side grinning at the baby and another woman who he seemed to remember being a cousin, the one who worked the winery, tried to coax Claire into handing over the baby. It took several minutes and a few more people coming in the front door for the majority of the family to settle back into their previous places.

The whole scene was foreign to Tucker. Most of the day, he'd worried about fitting in with the rich and somewhat famous. Especially since the Barons weren't just a little rich; these people had enough money to be running their own country. Now he was more concerned about fitting in with this large and affectionate family. As he sat in the chair nearest Claire still hogging the baby, he marveled at all the interactions. He wasn't sure he had ever been in the midst of such a big loving family. Any fool could see nothing about this home and family was relatable for a man who spent most of his life in a pick-up truck or a rodeo arena.

Slowly, as the family settled in and passed the baby around, rather than multiple small conversations, the entire room seemed to be engrossed in whether or not Devlin and Emily were only fooling themselves.

Having handed the baby over to her cousin Eve who had been the most recent member of the family to arrive, Claire leaned into him and whispered, "They really are just friends, but there's no convincing my grandfather of that."

He nodded. Not that he fully understood, but it was becoming clear to him that the Governor seemed to have one main agenda: marriage for the single grandchildren and children for the married ones. Now that was something he could relate to. Whether you were in a mansion or a doublewide, parents wanted marriage and grandchildren, in that order. He could actually hear his mother's voice in the back of his mind bemoaning when was he going to stop playing with horses and settle down. The memory almost made him laugh. Maybe the two very different worlds weren't so different at all.

CHAPTER ELEVEN

The look of abject horror on Tucker's face was enough to make Claire double over in laughter. Only years of practice at maintaining decorum at public events kept her from doing just that.

"Oh, you must have lots of practice with wee ones." Her cousin Siobhan grinned at the sight of Tucker cradling the newest Baron.

At least most of the color had returned to his cheeks. For a moment there, Claire had positioned herself to catch the baby just in case Tucker keeled over. She wasn't completely sure what prompted the exchange. One minute he was standing by her brothers at one side of the living room, laughing and talking horses and who knew what, when her grandmother, carrying little Beth, walked up to the band of single men. A moment later, she'd handed Tucker the small bundle and let go so fast that reflexes had him rolling the baby quickly up against his chest.

To Claire's surprise, she expected the baby to let out a nice and loud complaint at being passed off to someone who from the loss of all color from his complexion, clearly had limited, if any, experience handling babies. In years of veterinary practice, she'd come to learn that animal instincts were excellent at detecting fear and anxiety, and babies and little kids were pretty much the same. Any time she'd witnessed a nervous person take hold of an infant, before she could count the fingers on one hand, the baby would scream its protests until a confident soul took over. Usually mama.

Shaking her head, Leah dangled an arm across her shoulders. "That woman is just full of surprises."

It took Claire a moment to realize that her sister was looking at their grandmother.

"I can't swear to it," Leah sighed, "but I think the man just passed the latest litmus test."

Unfortunately, she knew exactly what her sibling referred to. Her grandfather had grown tired of waiting for his grandchildren to fall in love and it was not beneath him to try and find them matches to his liking. Since her cousins and siblings had begun a domino effect of marrying on their own, her grandparents, mostly her grandfather, had been less insistent on all of them finding soul mates, or so the remaining single grands had thought. Apparently, her grandparents were back on the find good spouses for the next generation kick, and she seemed to be on the top of the new list.

"Isn't it nice how well he does with babies?" It wasn't a question, exactly. Lila Baron smiled demurely and after patting her granddaughter on the shoulder, returned to her favorite chair with her dog contentedly at her side.

"Yep." Leah patted her sister on the forearm. "Passed the litmus test and you, my dear one, are the designated litmusee."

"Litmusee," she repeated softly after her sister's departing back. Was that even a real word?

Her gaze drifted to Tucker and the men all cooing at the baby. Siobhan, who stood slightly behind Tucker, wiggling her fingers at the baby, lifted her head and facing Claire only a few feet away, winked at her, cast a sideways glance at Tucker then again leveled her gaze with Claire and nodded.

Just what Claire didn't need, her family banding together to play matchmaker. Though, her gaze settling on Tucker now more comfortably cradling the baby in one arm while he tickled her cheek with the other, that thought made her warm and content all over. After all, Tucker was polite, thoughtful, smart, responsible, handsome, more than kind to animals, which was a big deal for Claire, and overall a really nice guy. Not a chauvinist jerk at all, simply a true gentleman.

"Do you want to hold her?" Tucker's gaze met hers.

Not till that second did she realize she'd been inching closer to Tucker and little Beth. "You seem to be enjoying her."

His eyes sparkled. "It's not what I expected."

"What?"

"Holding a baby."

At that second, while he spoke with her, he'd stopped fiddling with the baby. Little Beth reached out and grabbed hold of his extended finger.

Tucker's eyes popped and his smile shifted. Claire could almost see his heart melting. Heck, she wasn't the one holding the baby and the interaction between cowboy and baby had her heart turning to mush.

"Look at that." Cooper leaned forward, staring at the long finger engulfed in the tiny clenched fist. "Wow."

Shaking his head, his jaw slightly hanging, Tucker looked at Cooper. "This kid is crazy strong already."

"Her fingertips are almost white." Devlin frowned. "Is that normal?" His gaze lifted to meet Claire's.

"Why are you looking at me? I do animals, not people."

Devlin's frown deepened and a hint of panic settled in his gaze. "Where's Gwyneth?"

"Hang on." Claire extended her hand and placed it on her brother's forearm. "No need to bother Gwyneth. Beth is fine. It's normal for baby to latch on to a finger."

"She won't hurt herself?" Devlin's gaze shifted back to the baby and Claire had to bite her cheeks not to laugh at her brother's overreaction.

"I don't think it's bothering her." Now Tucker was smiling and shaking his head at the baby.

The amazing thing was how Beth's gaze followed Tucker's every move. Claire would pay big bucks for even a hint of what was going through the infant's mind.

"All right, everyone." Lila Baron stood clapped her hands. "Dinner is served."

The baby's nurse came from the kitchen and with practiced ease, received the baby from Tucker, and nodded to the adults huddled around, before hustling the little one upstairs to the nursery.

The thing that surprised Claire most was how, while everyone lumbered into the dining room, Tucker kept his gaze on the baby until the woman disappeared down the upstairs hall. How many more surprises would Tucker Pride have in store for her?

Dining with the Barons was everything he'd expected and at the same time, nothing like he'd expected.

The night of the cookout and bonfire, he'd had a wonderful time, but for the most part had been strictly an observer. He was enough of an extrovert not to have felt awkward, especially with everyone having been so welcoming, but tonight had been different. Tonight this massive family had succeeded in making him forget his ordinary world and feel a part of theirs. Tonight, he wasn't a cowhand, or another rodeo cowboy. He was one of them.

Though he suspected the silverware was really silver, that was the only thing that stood out as different. Brothers teased each other, cousins poked fun, sisters laughed, and more than once he found himself holding his own in the midst of the verbal sparring. It was the most fun he'd had at a large gathering in probably forever.

"This," he waved a finger at the pie, "is the best dessert I have ever had." Everything about the meal had been delicious. The pot roast and garlic mashed potatoes with sautéed asparagus reminded him of the comfort foods of grandmas and their apple pie, but this was something else. "What is it again?"

"Blueberry sour cream pie. It's one of Hazel's favorites. Her French toast casserole is right up there in the to-die-for category."

By the time he'd finished his last bite, he was beginning to fade, but the conversation around the table showed no sign of waning. Coffee was poured. The conversation continued and lifting his hand to his mouth, he did his best to disguise a yawn. He was hopeful no one noticed. Glancing around at the people happily eating and chatting around the crazy long table in the large room, he decided they had to all be night owls.

Claire's hand gently landed on his arm and the sparks shooting through him did a lot more to wake him up than the coffee ever would. "I'd like to check on Thunder before it gets much later. Join me?"

He glanced around the table, not wanting to offend his hosts by being the first to leave.

Among all her other qualities, it seemed Claire was also a mind reader. Before he could say a word, she smiled at him. "Don't worry," she spoke softly, "this is a working ranch. No one will hold it against you for checking on the horses. As a matter of fact, I wouldn't be surprised if Mitch didn't follow behind us."

Hiding another yawn, he nodded. Fresh air sounded really good about now.

Claire made their excuses and the moment the crisp air brushed his face, a second wind restored him.

In the barn he was delighted to see Thunder on his feet. "You are looking good."

"I thought you'd be happy. He's not favoring that leg at all." Claire stood beside him, stroking Thunder's neck as he looked his horse in the eye.

"You like it here, don't you?"

The horse nodded and whinnied.

"Yeah. I thought so." He couldn't blame the horse, he wasn't the only one learning to like life here more than he should. "How long before he can compete again?"

She shrugged. "I can't say, but I can tell you it's a good thing you're training with Star, because if you were thinking about Thunder for the championship, he's not even close to ready yet."

There was no way he was going to say that he wasn't thinking of the championships at all, he was thinking that every day they needed to delay moving on, the harder leaving would be.

"A penny for your thoughts?"

"Excuse me?"

Another shrug was accompanied by a soft chuckle. "You had an intense expression on your face. Being nosy, I wondered what had you so serious."

Still scratching the horse's neck, he tipped his head to see her better. "Do you know why this championship means so much to me?"

"Can't say that I do."

"I've been doing this a lot of years. When I was young, thinking of the future wasn't even the slightest consideration."

"You blew the money." There was no condemnation in her soft smile, just a statement.

"I did." No point in mentioning what on. "No one mentioned that thirty-year-old knees are less tolerant of stress than twenty-five-year-old knees."

She bobbed her head. "Same with backs and other joints."

"I smartened up, and started saving more than I spent. But if thirty is hard, thirty-five is worse and forty isn't going to be a picnic. I honestly feel like this is my last big shot at the brass ring."

"And what is that brass ring you want?"

His face lifted to the rafters and back. "Something like this would be the dream, but something more sensible would be attainable."

"Got something more sensible in mind?"

He patted the horse's neck. "There's a place not far from where I grew up in Wyoming. Lots of land. The house is falling apart, literally. Original owner passed away at least a decade ago. His heirs have been fighting over it ever since. Rumor has it that the estate is finally going to settle and the once upon a time ranch will be up for sale."

"Which is why this year is so important to you?"

"Yeah." He sighed. The all-important ranch that had felt so perfect for him, suddenly didn't seem to have the right fit. What he feared, is that after his time with Claire and the Barons, nothing would have the right fit again—ever.

So lost in his own thoughts, and doubts, he didn't notice

she'd stepped forward until her shoulder brushed against his. "You'll do it. Star's a good horse. You're a great roper. You've got this."

His gaze dropped to her arm against his. Thoughts of horses and ranches and roping slipped away. The only thing he could focus on was the sweet smell of vanilla in her hair and the rosy color of soft lips. "Claire?"

She blinked and dipped her chin, her voice low and sweet, "Yes?"

"I..." He shifted in place, set his free hand on her hip and leaned forward.

"There you are." Mitch's voice accompanied the squeak of the stall door hinges. "I figured you were either with Star or Thunder. Should have come here first."

"Star's my next stop." Tucker pulled his arm away from Claire and stroked the horse once again.

As Claire turned to face her cousin, Mitch's smile slipped and his gaze darted from her to Tucker and back. "Am I missing something?"

Claire shook her head. "Just talking championship rodeos."

"I see." Mitch did another glance from one to the other before smiling. "Since I was coming this way to check on a new foal, the Governor suggested I ask if Tucker might like to see some more of the ranch. Maybe take a ride tomorrow out to the original Paradise Ridge."

"Sounds nice." Tucker did like the idea of seeing more of the ranch, even if he never could afford anything like this place. "What time do you want to head out?"

"Oh," Mitch's smile widened, "not me." He turned to his cousin. "Our grandfather thought maybe you could take him out."

Tucker couldn't hold back his smile. One more reason to really like the old former Marine. A day on horseback with a beautiful woman who made the day brighter simply by entering the room. What more could a man ask for?

CHAPTER TWELVE

All night, Claire had debated where to take him on the ranch. To see it all, they'd need a four-wheeler. On horseback, they'd need a heck of a lot more than an afternoon. Only the King ranch had more land than Paradise Ridge.

"You ready?" Spatula in hand, Hazel spun around to face her. "I packed you a lunch. Mack has it down at the stables."

Just the thought of Hazel's picnic lunches was enough to make her stomach rumble with anticipation. Even if she'd finished breakfast less than an hour ago. "What'd ya make?"

"You know what I made."

"Fried chicken?" Hazel hardly ever made fried chicken for the family, but it was her favorite food source for picnics.

"That's right. No point in having cold lasagna, but cold fried chicken," the woman sighed, "perfect for an afternoon picnic."

"You're preaching to the choir."

That dragged a strong laugh from Hazel. "And you sing so pretty too."

Rolling her eyes, she shook her head and headed to the barn where she was due to meet Tucker. Just outside the stables, two horses were saddled and ready to go. Mack ran this ranch with the same skill and precision that her grandfather had run the Marine Corps. And to hear her grandfather talk, he apparently did indeed run the entire Corps without the help of anyone. Despite the iron will, or perhaps because of it, she really did adore both her grandparents.

"Morning." Dipping his chin, Tucker touched the brim of his hat in cowboy reverence.

"Morning." She smiled up at him. "You don't know it yet, but you're in for the best lunch of your life."

Mack stepped up beside her. "Ain't that the truth? Resisting the temptation to steal a piece just about killed me."

"You're not going to guilt me. I'll bet my last dollar that Hazel saved you more than one piece."

Their foreman's face broke into a huge smile. "Maybe I'll break for lunch early today."

"I bet there's more chicken at the ranch," Claire suggested with a glint in her eye.

"Not a bad idea. I'll head up as soon as I take care of a few things. Meantime, you two have a nice ride." With a wave, Mack turned and walked back into the barn.

Facing Tucker, Claire smiled. "Ready?"

"I've been looking forward to this ride since Mitch first mentioned it, but now I'm wondering if we shouldn't skip the ride and go straight to lunch?"

"It's only ten-thirty in the morning."

Tucker shrugged. "I've been around enough cowboys to know that when someone is that smitten with food, it's got to be good."

"And you'll find out at lunch time. Let's go or we'll never make it back before dark."

"If you insist." Another moment and they'd both mounted the horses and started a pleasant walk away from the ranch buildings.

"If you're wondering, your horse's name is Bourbon."

"Bourbon?"

"My cousin Paige wanted to name him Merlot and I think it was either Kyle or Craig who put their foot down and said it was too sissy a name for such a great work horse."

"So they named him Bourbon?"

She shook her head. "Actually, it was Eve who came up

with the Bourbon. She thought his coat reminded her of a glass of whiskey, but didn't like the sound of it. So he became Bourbon."

"And your horse?"

"This is Mabel. Sweetest work horse you'll ever meet. These are the best horses to get us up to the homestead and back without wearing out."

"Is it that far?"

Her head bobbed. "Closer if we were on four wheels instead of four legs."

At the bottom of the first hill, she tugged at her reins and pointed to the west. "I thought we'd start out at the original homestead cabin. It's the highest point on the ranch, you'll be able to see almost all of the original Conroe land. Then maybe we can make it by the caves at dusk."

"Conroe?"

"The ranch is from my grandmother's family. The Conroes."

"Ah. And there are caves here?"

"Nothing big and fancy. You can't even walk into them standing upright. It's really just a bunch of boulders that somehow formed a clump in the middle of nothing, but the bats call it home. They're fun to watch fly at dusk this time of year."

Tucker chuckled. "Okay, that was not what I expected."

"See? It's the surprises in life that make things interesting."

"Isn't that the truth." Tilting his head back, Tucker stared up. "One thing that never seems to surprise me is how blue the Texas sky can be. Back home, when the forecast says partly cloudy, we expect gray clouds to clutter the sky, possibly bring a storm or two. When the weather report here says partly cloudy, they mean expect a white cotton ball to float overhead. Clear and sunny growing up meant pretty blue with white puffs flowing by. Here, clear and sunny means bright and blue and not a puff of cloud to be seen with the naked eye."

"It is beautiful." She nodded. "Especially out here with nothing but green hills, scattered trees and the contented cows."

Tucker sputtered with laughter. "Anywhere else and I would argue the contented part, but here, I actually believe it."

She gave him the required tour monologue about the ranch size, the heads of cattle, the horses, and a few other trivialities such as how many fence posts are replaced or repaired annually. All the facts were peppered with occasional questions, jokes and all-around silliness. By the time they reached the hilltop, she felt as though they'd been friends all her life. "There." She pointed to her left.

They'd come close enough to see the cabin at the top of the hill.

Nudging Mabel to increase her walk to brisk trot, they reached the cabin in no time. Leaning forward, she waved one arm in an all-encompassing gesture, her finger dangling at the old log structure. "Welcome to the beginning of it all."

Situated up on a hill, the view from the cabin was beyond amazing. Not even in his dreams could he imagine owning a spread like this.

"Amazing, isn't it?" Claire spoke to him, but her gaze was on the rolling hills below. "As far as the eye can see is all Paradise Ridge."

Off in the distance, he spotted what looked like a small house below. "That house too?"

She squinted into the distance and nodded. "There are a handful of decent sized homes scattered about. The firstborn always inherited the main house. Grams was the only child of an only child, so she's always been in the big house. Other family members used to live on the land if they wanted to. Our foreman, Mack, lives in that house.

Not until this moment had it occurred to him that it must have been a challenge keeping this much land in the family. Considering how disagreeable heirs could be when there was serious money involved, it was a testament to the family history that the ranch was still intact for the next generation.

"Want to go inside?" she asked.

"Is it safe?" He felt her soft chuckle all the way down to his toes. Why did every little thing this woman did have such an impact on him?

"Grams wouldn't have it any other way." She lifted the massive iron lever on the original family cabin and pushed the door open.

In his mind, he expected to see broken and dust-covered furniture from a century ago. Perhaps an old cast-iron stove, but most definitely enough cobwebs for a horror movie. Instead, a warm cottage suitable for any magazine greeted him.

"Back when they built this cabin, dirt floors were the norm for most settlers. From the beginning my gazillion times great-grandfather built a home for his bride with wood floors. They were her pride and joy, her entire life."

Large solid logs gave the room texture. A small sofa was parked in front of a massive fireplace that had once upon a time most likely been used for cooking and heating the cabin. A rocker that he suspected was as old as the cabin was off to one side. A small table across the way had two chairs, neither of which looked to be as old as the rocker.

"Originally the cabin was just this room with the loft above." Claire pointed above, then turned to cross the room. "Once the children started coming, they added on a bedroom."

If he thought the main cabin was warm and welcoming, the bedroom was no exception. A brass bed decorated with quilts took up most of the space. A rocker similar to the one in the living room was in the corner and beside it, a small dresser with nothing but a gas lamp on it. "This is incredible."

As if punctuating his words, a loud clash sounded overhead. They both lifted their faces to the ceiling.

"I sure hope that's gunfire." Claire passed beside him. "Because I don't like the alternative."

With the wooden shutters of the bedroom closed, she

crossed the main room again and pulled open the door. He knew exactly what she was looking for. One thing he was very familiar with was the sound of gunshots and cars backfiring and the repeated crashing sound was neither.

"Dang it." Shaking her head while looking up, she sighed. "Where the hell did that come from?"

Standing beside her, he looked over her shoulder. A nasty storm was coming their way, fast. "Do you think we can make it back to the ranch house?"

Lips pressed tightly together, she shook her head.

He had no idea why he'd bothered asking. Considering how long it had taken to get here in the first place, he knew there was no way they'd make it back before the skies opened up and dumped rain all over them. Not that he minded getting wet, that was part of the working cowboy's life. The nasty sounding lightening above was what had him worried. "I don't think I've ever seen clouds move quite so fast."

"We'd better move the horses. There's a lean-to behind the cabin. That'll keep them dry and somewhat protected from the wind."

"I'll handle it."

"I'll come too. It will be faster." Quickly, they hurried out the door, the air crisp with electricity. If this sucker didn't blow past them, they were going to get a good downpour.

The horses secure, they rushed around to the front. Just as they unlatched the front door, the winds moving the clouds above blew around them, knocking his hat off. By the time he'd crossed the small space to grab his displaced hat, a flash of light lit the darkened sky seconds before a wall of rain came pouring down.

Claire sighed and with his help against the wind, shoved the door closed and bolted it. "Looks like we're not going anywhere." A small part of her had to admit, not a half-bad idea at all.

CHAPTER THIRTEEN

"So," Tucker glanced around, "now what?"

Claire wondered the same thing. Noticing the few homey touches her grandmother had added, she figured there could be worse places to be stuck during one of Texas's ever unpopular flash flood storms, especially when a storm's stalled and kept people stranded for days. "I suppose this will be as good a place as any to eat lunch."

"Good idea." Tucker smiled that sweet grin that warmed her all the way to her toes. "I admit breakfast feels like a long time ago."

"My tummy is letting me know I'm neglecting it too. Even though Grams keeps the place clean and stocked with supplies the same as we would a line shack. Just in case, well," she waved an arm, "something like this struck and the workers couldn't get home, but I think it's safe to say that we'll be happier with Hazel's fried chicken."

"No offense to your grandmother, but I've never seen a line shack anything like this."

"No offense taken, but I know what you mean." They had plenty of real line shacks. Most were just that, a shack. They might have a twin cot, a reasonable supply of canned goods, and running water, unlike this old cabin that relied on the hand pump at the sink. There had been plenty of discussions on tapping into the irrigation system for indoor plumbing, but Grams couldn't bring herself to modernize the cabin that much. Heck, it had taken years of arguing to agree to the loveseat instead of the pair of rockers.

Another clash of thunder sounded, this one closer than the last, and Tucker glanced up as if he could see through the roof. "I'd better hurry and get the food." He reached for the door latch as a gust of wind shoved the door open. "If this wind keeps up, the storm should be halfway to Nebraska by the time we're done eating."

In a short time, Claire had the coffee table in front of the small love seat laid out with a feast fit for a king. "The sofa is more comfortable than on the grass, but this feels more picnic like than eating at the table."

"Not to mention all this food wouldn't fit on that little table." Tucker pointed to the two seater wooden café table across the small room.

Legs crossed and a paper plate of food on her lap, Claire faced him as she picked at a piece of chicken. Her curiosity had been getting the best of her. "What are your plans after the finals?"

Swallowing his food, he stared at the half-eaten piece of chicken. "I suppose it depends on how the finals go. Sam has been talking about retiring for years. I think win or lose, this year is it for him."

"And you? Will this be your last year?" Casually, she pulled at a piece of cornbread, pretending she wasn't hanging on his every word.

He shrugged. "My mind tells me that I can learn to work with another wrangler. Compete for a lot more years. My heart, and my joints, are quick to point out that I can't keep doing this forever."

"I know how that feels. My mind is always thinking, yeah, I can party all night and go to work the next day, and once ten o'clock rolls around the rest of me is shouting, *girl, go home and get some sleep*!"

That made him chuckle. "My body shouts a lot more than that at me after an afternoon of roping events."

No way was she touching that comment with a ten-foot pole. The less she knew about Tucker's body the better off they'd all be.

"What about you?" He set down his cleaned chicken bone on the table, and took a sip of the lemonade Hazel had packed before leaning against the sofa back. "Any unfulfilled dreams?"

Her plate empty, Claire leaned forward and set the dish

on the table beside his before settling back on the sofa. "Honestly, I don't know."

"How can you not know?"

"As a little kid, I wanted to be a princess with a knight in shining armor to whisk me away to his castle. Not that I actually understood what all that meant when I was five. By the time I started school, fairytale dreams slipped away and all I wanted was to take care of animals. As you can see, that dream stuck. But now that I'm all grown up, the stress of school is way behind me, and I love what I do, there doesn't seem to be any time to stop and think of the next dream." One shoulder hefted in a lazy shrug. "Guess that sounds silly."

"Not at all." He slowly shook his head. "My granddad used to say, find something you love to do and you'll never work a day in your life."

"What did your grandfather do?"

"He was a chauffeur for some crazy rich family. Oil money, I think. Anyhow, Granddad loved to read. So, he found a job where he could sit in a car and read until he had to take his bosses somewhere else, and then he'd wait and read some more. He was quite happy."

"And you? What makes you happy?"

"I love horses, and I love riding, and I love roping, but it's a lot harder on a body than reading."

"Tell me about it. After that little sideshow for my future nieces, my muscles protested loudly for days."

Again, he chuckled softly. "See what I mean?"

A flash of light seeped through the cracks of the closed shutters, followed quickly by a loud rumble of thunder. Just the sound chilled her to the bone. Rubbing her hands briskly against her arms, she tried to brush the chill away.

"Cold?"

"A little."

Tucker inched closer and tugged her against him, wrapping one arm around her. "I don't have a jacket to lend you."

"This is nicer." She snuggled into him. No need to mention among other things stocked in the small bedroom was a cedar chest with linens and blankets. After all, how stupid would she be to point that out?

Nicer was one word for the feel of Claire tucked snuggly against him. He'd been aching to hold her for some time, and now that she was here with him, he would be hard pressed to let go.

Another bolt of lightning flashed, only this time the thunder was delayed a few seconds. "Sounds like the storm isn't as close."

"It will probably blow by soon."

And wasn't that just a dang shame. He found himself in no hurry to leave. Staying here, curled up in front of the fireplace with Claire, even if it wasn't lit, held a great deal of appeal. "Maybe. I'm sorry I didn't know the storm was going to blow in."

"It's not your fault. That bright blue cloudless sky gave no inkling that stormageddon was blustering in." Under any other circumstances, having his plans turned upside down by unexpected weather might have been more than off-putting, but what kind of idiot would he have to be to object to being stranded—even temporarily—alone in a cozy cabin with a beautiful woman?

"I can't help but feel a little responsible."

"Don't." With a will of their own, his fingers began drawing lazy circles on her arm.

Still tucked against him, Claire lifted her chin to see him. "If you win the grand prize at nationals and you buy that land, think you'll just hang up your rodeo spurs?"

"Good question." Even if he could afford the land he'd been eyeing for the last couple of years, the more time he spent with the Barons, the more the need to put down roots in one place was taking hold of him. The problem he faced now, for the first time ever, planting those roots in Texas instead of Wyoming or Montana was starting to hold way more appeal than it would have just a short month ago. "I never was a very good planner, but from where I'm sitting, this hilltop is feeling pretty nice."

"The hilltop?" Her head tipped back ever so slightly to better see him, or were her eyes saying something more?

The temptation to pick up where Mitch interrupted last night had been building in him from the moment she sat across from him and dug into the fried chicken. Whether or not it had been the best he'd ever tasted, he had no idea. All he could focus on was the delicate way her fingers pulled at the chicken and then how her lips sucked at her fingertips, removing all traces of grease.

"Tucker? Did I lose you?" Her brows buckled over eyes that held confusion.

"Not a chance." Chucking chivalry to the wind, he shifted his weight and praying he hadn't read her wrong, pulled her even closer, letting his lips descend on hers.

The first touch sent sparks shooting down his spine. The feel of her was everything he had expected, and so much more. As if made for him, and only him, she melted against him, the perfect fit. The kiss grew longer, and stronger, and suddenly the storm, the wind, and the rest of the world faded away. He didn't dare move his hands, every fiber of his being shouted that he'd want more than he had a right to.

Another crash of thunder sounded, only softer and farther away. How he wanted to shout for the storm to come back, to stay, so he could keep Claire in his arms. Her fingers began toying with his hair at the back of his head and he couldn't help but pull her impossibly closer. Another shift, and he was splayed across the small sofa with Claire practically sprawled on top of him.

As wonderful as it felt to have so much of her so close to him, this was so not a good idea. Regretting it more than he wanted to admit, he eased his head back and sucked in a long breath. Somewhere, the lord above must have given him an approving pat on the back as her cell phone rang, forcing her to sit up right and slip the phone out of her back pocket.

"Hi, Grams."

"I've been trying to reach you for over an hour. Are you two okay? Do I need to send out a rescue party?"

Smiling at him, Claire eased off his legs and settled into the sofa cushion. "We're holed up at the homestead. It sounds like the storm is blowing by already."

"Yes. It's clear as day here again, but there's going to be a lot of mud out there. If you sense it's too much for the horses to make their way back, just call and we'll send out a four-wheeler."

"I can go now." She recognized her brother Cooper's voice, followed by Devlin. "Horses, my foot. We'll go get them."

"And what will you do with the poor horses?" Her grandmother shot back at her brothers. The rest of the conversation was muffled, but another minute and Grams was back. "You're a big girl. You can handle yourself. But if things don't go well—"

"I'll call. Promise."

The two said their I love yous and good byes and Tucker couldn't help but think there wasn't a blessed thing in Wyoming that could compete with this little cabin, and this beautiful woman. The question at hand was the same, win or lose, what the heck was he going to do next?

CHAPTER FOURTEEN

There was no way that Claire was missing out on today's rodeo. Tucker had been calm, yet restless for the last couple of days. She couldn't blame him. As the big day drew closer, she was feeling more antsy and anxious and she wasn't going to be the one competing.

Even though the sun was barely winking over the horizon, she was wide awake, showered, dressed and waiting for the rest of the world to rise and shine. Making her way downstairs, she, of course, found Hazel in the kitchen. "Morning."

"My, my, you are up early." Bowl in hand, Hazel looked up from stirring. "You beat your grandfather downstairs."

"Couldn't sleep."

"It's a big day." Hazel returned to beating the contents of the bowl. "Pancakes will be ready in a bit. Bacon's in the oven. I'll have the eggs started in a few. I bet you're not the only one up early." One side of her face listed in a sweet smile, one that said, *I have a secret.* Not that her budding relationship with Tucker was a secret to anyone with eyes.

Nervous about today, but happier than she'd been in forever, Claire reached for one of Hazel's fresh biscuits. Two could play this game. "You're up early."

Rolling her eyes, Hazel nudged the butter in Claire's direction then went back to stirring the batter. "I did not mean me and you know it. But if you're curious, might I suggest you check out the barn?"

The barn. Made sense that Tucker would be having a morning visit with Star. This would be a big day for both of them. "I think I'll see how my star patient is doing."

A smile as wide as Hazel's face bloomed. "You go ahead and do that."

It only took a few minutes to reach the stables. In the morning silence, she could hear Tucker softly speaking to Thunder. She'd actually expected to find him in the other section, but it made sense that he would be consoling his best friend on the big day that Tucker would share with another horse. By now, she thought she'd learned so much about that man, and yet, every day there was something new to discover. Today was merely another opportunity to see his tender heart. Scared to death or not, there was no denying what the man did to her.

If she'd had any doubt of her feelings for him, they were completely erased at the sight of him standing gently by his beloved horse, murmuring softly. Ever since the day they'd been stranded in the cabin for those few short hours, they'd shared an awful lot of hand-holding, stolen kisses, long walks, and had talked about everything and anything that came to mind—except what would happen to him, his horse and them, after today's championship.

"Thought that might be you." Tucker shifted his gaze from the horse to her and broke into a soul melting smile.

"I could have been Mack." She smiled back. A smile that came easily whenever he looked at her with those beautiful deep blue eyes.

He shook his head and stepped away from the horse. "Nah, he has a heavier gait and stomps his left foot."

Surprise smacked her. "Are you serious?"

"Absolutely. Your steps are always slower, measured, but strong and purposeful." Stepping into her personal space, he leaned in and captured her lips in a brief, sweet kiss. "A lot like you."

Taking hold of his hands in hers, she stared up at him. "You can determine all that from a person walking a few feet?"

He nodded and shrugged. "It's a gift."

That had her laughing. A lot of the things he did and said made her laugh. More than anyone else she'd ever dated. Probably more than any friend she'd ever had. That thought made her smile. And even though he knew the family had money, there wasn't a thing about him that indicated he was interested in her bank account. They were friends. She liked that. Yes, she wanted more, but her grandmother always insisted that good friends made the best soul mates and life partners. She wanted that right now more than she'd ever thought possible. Scared or not, she was most definitely, and absolutely, head over heels in love with that man.

The minute Tucker heard Claire's footsteps approach, his heart did a somersault. He'd almost gotten used to the way everything about him got all revved up whenever she came near. Since that afternoon in the cabin, he'd tried his best to convince himself that the way she made him feel was nothing special, nothing different, that in time, like all other infatuations and flirtations, this feeling would pass. And every time he saw her, his heart laughed at him like a loon.

Tossing and turning all night, he reminded himself that Star was a fantastic horse who moved with him as if they had been riding together for years, and repeatedly told himself that today would be fine. That all his dreams and aspirations could come true if he clinched the day. And then he'd realize that without Claire, none of those dreams meant a damn thing to him and roll over and try to sleep some more. In the end, like it or not, poor timing or not, there was only one conclusion to be had: he was most definitely head over boot heels in love with that tenderhearted blonde. He should have realized exactly how special she was when Thunder cottoned to her as if she had been his long last mother.

As much as he wanted to pull her against him and kiss her silly, today was a big day. Nationals were a two-hour drive from the ranch and he needed to get Star settled in and rested from the trip before the rodeo started. Kissing the only woman he'd truly ever loved would have to wait.

"Are you ready?" Her smile was so darn distracting.

"As ready as I'll ever be."

"Guess it's time to load Star and get moving." She glanced over his shoulder at her patient. "He really is doing great. Coming along faster than I thought."

Patting Thunder's neck, Tucker nodded. "I feel awful that we're not going to do this together, but no prize is worth risking Thunder."

Another short while and they had Star secured and ready to go. From the way he almost loaded himself into the trailer, it was obvious to anyone that the horse was as excited as they were. If anyone were to ask her, she'd have to say that she truly believed Star knew where they were going and was as determined as Tucker to win.

"Are you sure you want to come with us? It's going to be a very long day."

"I know." She flashed that irresistible smile. "I want to be there with both of you."

Oh, how he loved her for saying that. Words wouldn't come to describe how very grateful he was for her support. "Then I guess we're off."

Settled in the truck, the conversation seemed to easily ramble from topic to topic, the same as it did every time they were together. A few times, silence hovered, and he understood better than ever the concept of comfortable silence. What he couldn't understand was how come some smart, competent man had not caught this amazing woman.

"Are you worried about the events?" Concern showed in her eyes.

"No more than usual." Normally at this point his mind would be all over the upcoming finals, but he most definitely had something else—someone else—on his mind.

"You look awfully serious," she prodded.

"Just thinking."

"About?"

Taking his eyes off the road a moment, he glanced at her leaning against the passenger door and staring at him. "Truth?"

"Always."

"Why haven't you ever married?" The minute a dark curtain descended over her normally bright eyes, he regretted butting his nose in where it didn't belong. "Sorry. That's none of my business."

"It's a reasonable question, though I will point out the days of the little woman finding a man to make her happy is very much the last millennium."

"Understood." He bobbed his head. "Is that the more polite way of reminding me that I'm a chauvinist?"

Her shoulders shaking, she laughed loudly. "Maybe." Another curtain descended and all humor slid away from her eyes. "There are challenges that come from being a member of a well-recognized family. Especially one with a lot of money."

Oh, he so didn't like where this conversation was going. He had to force himself to loosen his grip on the steering wheel.

"Some guys were nice enough, no big deal, but lately, I seem to have had more than my share of jerks more interested in my family, and the money that comes with it, than in me."

"I'm sorry."

"Why? It's not your fault most men are jerks."

As much as he'd love to argue that point, he knew an awful lot of guys, especially on the circuit, who qualified as bona fide jerks. He probably even knew a few who would have gladly made a play for Claire just for the money that came with the girl. Without thinking, he stretched out his hand and curled it over her nearest hand. "I think jerk is too kind a word for those idiots who let you get away."

She shrugged. "Honestly, there wasn't a single one who had my interest, not enough to be thinking forever and a day, but lately there seemed to be more gold diggers than usual."

"I thought gold diggers was an expression reserved for women?"

One brow rose up on her forehead and she shot him a piercing glare.

"Chauvinist?"

She chuckled heartily. "Just a little."

"Point taken. I'll try to be less predictable."

"Sounds good." Her fingers threaded with his and they held on to each other until he pulled into the parking lot, found his designated spot, and was forced to let go in order to unload Star. The downside of his stupid question—now more than ever, he had to win that prize. Without it, how could she ever believe he loved her for who she was and not her family's money?

CHAPTER FIFTEEN

A grin as wide as the Rio Grande on his face, an older man with cowboy swagger if Claire had ever seen one came waltzing up to them and slapped Tucker on the back. "You made it."

"Like there's anything on this planet that could keep me away." Slapping each other on the back the way men often did, Tucker turned to her. "This is Sam. Best team roper on the planet."

The man shrugged. "That might be a teeny bit of an exaggeration." He tipped his hat. "You must be this character's guardian angel."

"I beg your pardon?" She thought of herself as a lot of things, but a guardian angel had never been one of them.

"I hear you saved Thunder's leg and found this guy a great horse to replace him."

"Thunder can't be replaced." Tucker's lips thinned and tightened.

"Hey. You know what I mean."

Without a word, Tucker gave a small nod.

"Let's see this horse you're riding." Sam waved at the trailer.

As soon as Tucker had opened the closure and walked the horse out, Sam whistled.

"He's a beauty, isn't he?" Tucker's smile returned.

"If he rides as good as he looks, we've got this all sewn up." Sam smiled at the horse who eyed him intently.

Sensing Star was not completely comfortable with all the attention, Claire inched forward and stroked the animal's neck. "It's all right, boy. Soon you'll be able to show your stuff to the world."

The horse bobbed his head and Claire couldn't help but smile. Horses were so much smarter than the average person gave them credit for.

Stalls were assigned to the two men, side by side. There was still time before everything started and Hazel and the rest of her family arrived to cheer Tucker on. Claire had no idea how the guys were feeling, but she had butterflies in her stomach entertaining themselves by dive bombing over and over. Even back when she was competing, she never felt like this.

"It's still early." Sam tossed the brush he'd been using on his horse into a nearby bucket. "What do you say we grab a bite to eat?"

"The restaurant isn't open yet." Tucker frowned.

Sam shook his head. "No, but there's a food truck in the back parking lot. Great Mexican street corn."

"What did the doc tell you about spicy foods?"

"Not a blessed thing. I'm supposed to watch my cholesterol. I haven't had fried chicken in over a month. There's no cholesterol in corn."

"It's not the corn I'm worried about." Tucker began walking in the same direction as Sam. "It's all the fried foods that will probably go with the corn."

Sam looked over his shoulder and shot them a toothy grin. "Yeah."

The casual camaraderie was more entertaining than prime time television. If the two worked this well together in the arena, Tucker would be right, they'd have it made in the shade.

Seated at one of the few scattered picnic tables, Claire had opted for the truck that served Philly cheese steaks, Tucker chose a slice of pizza with extra cheese claiming he didn't like to eat much before a competition, but he'd nailed Sam a thousand percent correctly. The guy had his plate filled with Mexican cuisine, from greasy tacos, too much hot sauce, nachos and the coveted street corn. How the man was as skinny as he was, Claire didn't understand.

"How much hot sauce are you going to put on that?" Tucker's eyes were almost falling out of his head as he watched Sam shake more and more spicy hot sauce onto his tacos.

Sam shrugged. "I'm from Louisiana, I was weaned on this stuff."

The way he began sweating, Claire had her doubts that the man wasn't oblivious to his own limits. When Sam popped several acid relief tablets in his mouth as if they were candy, not once but twice, she found herself watching him more closely.

While Sam took a moment between bites to wipe his mouth and his brow with the nearby paper napkin, Claire leaned into Tucker. "Does he always eat like this before a competition?"

On a heavy sigh, Tucker nodded. "Afraid so."

"And the hot sauce always makes him sweat?"

"No." Tucker frowned, suddenly looking at his friend with new eyes. Focusing on his friend, Tucker left half the pizza on his plate. "You feeling all right, buddy?"

Sam nodded, and reached for more antacids.

Shaking his head, Tucker looked around. "I don't think so, Sam."

"Of course I'm…fi…ne." And just like that he grabbed his chest with his left hand, and slapped his other hand over it.

"Shit." Claire sprang from her seat and ran around the table. "Alert security. We need medical."

Tucker was on his phone. Claire quickly took the man's pulse. Aw hell, 150 beats per minute. She didn't need to be a people doctor to know that Sam was sitting dead smack in heart attack territory. This would be so much easier if Sam weren't a human. Pulling off her sweatshirt, she balled it into a pillow and laid it on the bench. "Sam, lie down. We need to get your heart rate down."

"I'm fine," the man grumbled, still holding his chest.

Stubborn man.

"Medical team is on their way." Tucker slid his phone into his pocket, and smiling at his friend who had finally agreed to lie down, shook his head. "I told you all that hot sauce was going to get you one of these days."

"Nonsense," the man barked at him, "I'll be fine in a few minutes. We have a championship to win."

Tucker's smile slipped for a moment and Claire spotted the flash of disappointing recognition in his eyes. "Not today, Sam."

"Hell, yes." Sam struggled to sit up. His face scrunching and his hand pushing hard against his chest.

"Damn it, Sam," Tucker growled at his friend. "Lay the hell down and behave."

Before he could say anything else, the med team came running over. Claire had never been so happy to see a human doctor in her life. Taking a step back, she let the people do their thing. One man had a blood pressure cuff on Sam and the doctor had a stethoscope in his ear and on Sam's chest.

His arm around her waist, Tucker kissed the top of her head. "Thanks for noticing he was in trouble."

"I didn't do anything."

"Yes. You had me calling for help. I'm sure I would have realized, but it might have taken me a few more minutes and I have a feeling that those few minutes may be critical."

At those words, the doctor set up an IV, and injected something into Sam's arm.

"Get this dang thing off of me. I have a championship to ride."

"You're in cardiac arrest. You are not riding anything except in that ambulance to the ER." The doctor pointed to the vehicle pulling up.

Sam's gaze drifted to Tucker.

Without hesitation, Tucker nodded at the old man. "Go. You're more important than any buckle."

Another few moments and Sam was safely inside the ambulance and on his way to the hospital with reassurances from the EMTs that he was out of danger.

"I guess we should ride over. Do you know who has his medical power of attorney?" When Tucker didn't say a word, she looked up at him. "Why are you staring at me like that?"

That lazy smile that had her from day one, slowly took over his face. "You're going to take Sam's place."

Deer in the headlights didn't quite describe the shocked look on Claire's face, but it came pretty darn close. "Don't look at me like I've lost my mind."

Snapping her dropped jaw shut, she blinked hard. "Unless you mean something other than me replacing Sam in team roping, then you have indeed lost your mind."

"Think about it."

Shaking her head and waving her arms, she took a step back, followed by another. "I don't need to think about it. I already know. You've lost your mind."

"You're good."

"I've never team roped in my life," she practically shouted at him.

"I saw you roping the practice steer. You didn't miss."

"Both of us were stationary. You're talking about riding a racing horse and roping a steer that's thinks it's running for its life."

"It's no different than those barrels you raced around."

Her eyes popped open even wider. "The barrels don't move."

"You can do this. I know you can."

She continued shaking her head at him. "I've never even been on Sam's horse."

The slow pressure building in his chest at the realization that his one chance to be worthy of Claire was slipping away eased at the sound of those words. The frantic panic in her eyes had dissipated and her voice had softened. She was considering it. "He's a good horse."

"This is crazy. You can't win with me."

"And I won't win without you. What have we got to lose?" He could almost see the wheels turning in her still shaking head.

"Look at this." She lifted her hands, palms up. "Just

thinking about it and I'm sweating like I'm going to be the next cardiac case."

"Don't say that." He pulled her into his arms and tucked her head against his shoulder. "Don't even think such a horrible thing. Nerves are normal, and you are so very good at everything you do."

"But this is so important to you." Pulling back, she lifted her gaze to meet his.

His finger under her chin, he studied her face. Could see the fear. Not about riding—that had to be as second nature as breathing for her—but at letting him down. "The most important thing to me is you. If you really don't want to do this, then we don't do it. I pack up my saddle and walk away. Nothing matters more to me than you. Nothing."

Blinking at him, it took a long moment, but a small smile teased at her the corners of her mouth. "You won't hate me?"

"Never in a million years."

Bobbing her head, she stepped out of his hold. "I'm not saying yes, but let me at least meet Sam's horse."

"Done." Stretching his hand out, he snatched hers into his. With every step, he could feel the tension building exponentially as they drew closer.

"I must be out of my mind for even considering this." Her fingers dug into his knuckles.

A few more steps and they stood in front of Gray's stall. Tucker took in a deep breath and said a fast prayer. "Here he is."

Slowly, she approached the horse whose eyes followed her slow steady moves. "Well, hello boy."

Turning his head slightly, the horse continued to follow her with his eyes.

"Sam's had a little incident." She stroked the horse's jaw. "Tucker here thinks I can ride you."

"He's a little bigger than Thunder."

She nodded. "You're a strong boy, aren't you?"

The horse seemed to be studying her every move and considering her every word.

"Do you think we can do this?" she asked the animal.

Some days, Tucker swore horses were way smarter than humans. The gentle giant turned to look at Tucker, then turned back to Claire and nodded.

Blowing out a long slow breath, Claire leveled her gaze with Tucker's. "Looks like we're doing this."

CHAPTER SIXTEEN

Now Claire wasn't sure who was crazier, Tucker for suggesting she ride with him instead of Sam, or her for agreeing to this insane idea. Talking to the steel gray animal, she needed to bond with this boy and fast. She hoped that brushing him down worked to bribe the horse into being nice to her. Or at least forgiving.

She murmured softly to Gray as she stroked him and wondered if Tucker was having a challenge convincing the powers that be to allow her to replace Sam on his horse. A part of her almost hoped that the last-minute change wouldn't be allowed. That would solve the problem of her letting him down. With every passing minute, she became more nervous. Other than a couple of weeks ago when she'd demonstrated roping for Michelle, she hadn't done any competitive roping. Yep, she was definitely bonkers for agreeing to this.

"It's done." Tucker came up to her, smiling, and carrying a number for her to attach to her shirt back. "Thankfully, because you're on Sam's horse and we're registered as a team, not as individuals, the substitution is allowed."

"Marvy." She knew her smile couldn't look sincere. But what was it her grandmother used to say to her as a child? Keep smiling and eventually you'll believe it yourself.

"There is one caveat."

"Only one?" She could think of a lot of pitfalls to this crazy idea.

"If anyone files a formal protest, it could put a snag in the final results."

"And when will these protests happen?"

He shrugged. "Any time, but my guess? When we win."

When? Oh, this guy had too much faith in her. All she could think was how much it was going to hurt when she blew the preliminary round and came crashing off that pedestal he'd put her on.

"Now, I need to ask you. Do you want to heel or head? I can do either."

It took her a moment to register what he wanted to know. She hadn't even considered if Sam roped the horns or the feet. "I'm not sure."

His brows rose high on his forehead and for the first time since proposing this hare-brained idea, he looked concerned.

"I haven't tried to rope a steer's hooves since youth rodeo. Though, I don't know if a three tries at a stationary practice steer counts for much more." If she really had her druthers, she'd be in the stands as a spectator, but obviously that ship had sailed.

His expression didn't change as she voiced her thoughts out loud.

"If you rope a horn and nose, or two horns or the head, there are no point deductions?"

"Correct."

"But if I only get one foot, then we lose points?"

"Five," he answered.

Yep. Definitely header. At least she had a three in one shot of getting it right and only two as a heeler and one of those would lose them five points. Then again, if he missed all together with the horns, then they were out and she didn't have to do anything. Some days she really hated making decisions. "Okay." She nodded and breathed in deeply. "Heeler."

He bobbed his head. "Heeler it is."

Patting the horse's rump, she glanced over at Sam's saddle. Lord help her. "Let's get this show on the road."

Not for the first time, Tucker considered putting Claire through this might be the most selfish thing he'd ever done. If he wanted to win, he really didn't have any other choices. And if he didn't win, how would Claire ever be sure it wasn't her money he was after? The cliché between a rock and a hard place had never been more real for him.

Claire refused to let him help her saddle Gray. Something about part of the bonding. "Ready, boy?" She placed a foot in the stirrup and seemed to wait for Gray's reaction. The animal didn't move. "I'll take that as a yes." Just as she pushed up, the horse turned to look at her and rocked back on one foot. "Okay." She eased back down. "We need to come to terms with each other here."

Tucker came within an inch of calling the whole thing off. "Claire…"

Her head whipped around to face him and rather than fear, he saw determination and a definite message of *back off*. The look reminded him of the expression when she'd been goaded into demonstrating barrel racing the other week. This was no longer giving in to help him, it was now something she had to prove to herself. Lord, how he loved this woman's spirit.

Back to facing the horse, she held on to the saddle horn and stared at Gray. "Let's do this once more." This time her leg swung up and over and the horse didn't budge. A huge smile took over her face. Not a shaky nervous smile, but a sincere grin of satisfaction.

Now came the hard part—earning enough points to take the championship and have the purse all to themselves.

On their mounts, awaiting their cue, Tucker and Claire watched his closest competition this season thunder forward after the frantic steer. The header twirled the rope above him before expertly snagging both horns. The heeler racing up to the steer let his rope fly and captured one hoof. Only one. Yes! A five point deduction. His excitement kicked up a notch. Stealing a moment to glance at Claire, he saw the same delight in her expression. She knew exactly what this meant. If neither of them made a mistake, they'd hold the top spot for the next round.

Anticipation and nerves battled each other as he continued debating if pushing Claire to replace Sam had been a brilliant move or the biggest mistake of his life. The signal given, they were up next. He and Claire positioned themselves on either side of the chute. Star, the horse with the eye of eagles, exuded the calm strength that he'd hoped for. Across the way, Claire held her focus with no signs of nervous jitters. Watching for any signs of rebellion from Sam's trusted horse, relief washed over him at Gray's steadiness. The last thing they needed was for Gray to fight his new rider.

The do-or-die moment upon them, Tucker's heart pounded in his chest as he reminded himself to breathe. The weight of expectation was heavy on his shoulders. The announcer's voice boomed through the arena. His muscles coiled like a spring ready to burst free. As he and Star bolted forward, adrenaline coursed through Tucker's veins. The thunder of hooves echoed in his ears. The world around him narrowed to a single point of focus—the steer racing ahead. More than see her, he could feel Claire keeping pace with him, zooming across the arena. The same as with Sam, he knew she'd be positioned exactly where she needed to be. The rope in his hand, the rhythm of Star's powerful strides beneath him as if they were one, with split-second precision, Tucker swung his rope. The loop sliced through the air and circling around both horns, yanked the animal to sudden near stop.

This was it, everything hinged on Claire. Time suddenly seemed to come to a screeching halt. The roar of the crowd gave way to the almost deafening pounding of his heart in his ears. His vision momentarily blurred, the arena slipped into slow motion. He cut around in an effort to keep the rope taut and stop the steer from dancing a jig that would make it harder for her to hit her mark. Twirling the rope as they closed in on the animal, Claire and Gray thundered into position. The steer struggled in place as the rope fell toward the writhing animal, caught its target and tightening around both rear hooves, brought the battling animal to the ground. Despite the dizzying sensation of time passing at the pace of a distressed snail, according to the clock, they'd made as good time as any of his and Sam's best performances.

They'd done it. Claire had done it. The crowd on their feet, the two trotted out of the arena. When the horses came to a stop and they dismounted, her smile as bright as a ray of sunshine, Claire scurried around Gray and flung herself at him.

Circling his arms around her, Tucker hauled Claire against him. With her legs wrapped around his hips, her lips tight against his, he'd give up all the money in the world to make her this happy, this joyful, this proud. The sound of a throat clearing snapped them out of their revelry.

"Oops," she softly muttered as she slid down, her feet landing steadily on the ground. "We'd better get out of the way."

She looked so darn precious when she was embarrassed, but she also looked downright sultry, glowing from the adrenaline rush.

"I can't believe I did it." Heaving a heavy sigh, her shoulders shuddered with a silent squeal. "We actually did it."

"We did." He took the lead and started down the path to their stalls. "Now only ten more rounds to go."

Mouth open, she whipped around to face him, and kicking her head back, she groaned so loud half the cowboys turned to stare. He really did love that woman.

CHAPTER SEVENTEEN

The next few days were insane. Claire had to scramble to clear her schedule in order to continue competing. Much to her surprise, no one objected to the last-minute substitution. She suspected the lack of discontent was more a matter of respect for Sam than acceptance of her on the team.

The other thing that surprised the dickens out of her was how much fun she'd had. That first rush of adrenaline as she soared through the arena and actually managed to rope not one but both hooves on the small steer was almost as exciting as saving a mama and her baby in a rough delivery.

But nothing beat seeing their names at the top of the boards. Her stomach twisted every time another team tore into the arena and executed a near flawless example of team roping. For days, her heart had been pounding, and with every point they gained, her cheeks hurt from so much smiling. When the winners were finally announced, her family and friends hooted and hollered louder than the rest of the arena combined. For her the money didn't matter. She'd already agreed to give her part to Sam. After all, he'd done all the work with Tucker to get them to the finals in the first place.

Now, it felt odd after all the excitement, to be sitting casually around a table the same as any other Sunday afternoon.

"Is there any salt on the table?" Cooper looked around.

"Here you go." Devlin handed his brother the salt. "How come Hazel's never made this soup before?"

"Hazel didn't make it." Grams dipped her spoon into the steaming bowl.

Several heads at the Baron dining table popped up. The kitchen had been Hazel's domain for so many years, no one expected anyone else to cook. Ever.

"Wait." Leah stared down at the bowl. "Who cooked this?"

Grinning, Claire waved a thumb at Tucker seated beside her.

All eyes shifted in the cowboy's direction.

"Y'all just got home from nationals, what…?" Cooper glanced down at his watch. "Three hours ago. When did you find time to make soup?"

"I have a better question." Her cousin Eve waved a finger at Tucker. "How'd you get Hazel to let you cook in her kitchen?"

At that moment, Hazel came out of the kitchen carrying a second tray of grilled corn on the cob. "The man just won the National Rodeo Championship. He's earned the right to do whatever he wants." The woman shrugged. "Not my fault all he seemed to want was to cook."

"Frankly," Cooper dipped his spoon into the bowl again, "I don't particularly care who cooked it, this stuff is the best chicken tortilla soup I've ever had."

"Ditto," multiple voices chorused.

Shaking her head, Hazel leaned into Tucker. "You're going to have to give me the recipe. I can never get some of these youngins to eat their vegetables."

"Vegetables?" One of the younger cousins looked down at his soup. "How many vegetables?"

Holding up one hand, Tucker counted off. "Cabbage, corn, onion, broccoli, celery, red pepper and green pepper. That makes seven."

A few of the younger cousins glared cross-eyed at the soup.

Justin, the teen who asked what vegetables, looked up at Tucker. "You're sure there's cabbage in this? I don't like cabbage."

Tipping his head to one side, Tucker smiled at the younger cousin. "But you like the soup?"

Justin nodded.

"Then what difference does it make what's in it?" Tucker had a brilliant way of rationalizing the irrational. After all, he convinced Claire to compete with him.

Staring down at the bowl begrudgingly, her cousin seemed to make up his mind. With a lazy shrug, he dug his spoon into the bowl again. "I guess."

"See?" Hazel winked at Tucker and turning on her heel, marched back into the kitchen.

"Still thinking of buying property in…" The Governor narrowed his gaze in thought. "Montana?"

"Wyoming," Claire corrected. She hadn't had the nerve to ask Tucker the same question. In some ways she seemed to be in ostrich mode. If she buried her head in the sand and didn't discuss the winnings and the land in Wyoming, then maybe it would all just go away and he'd stay here with her.

"Well," Tucker sucked in a deep breath, "I'm not really sure."

"Oh," Grams smiled, "why is that?"

"For one thing," Tucker toyed with the spoon handle, "Thunder still has more recovery time ahead of him."

Thank heaven for Thunder. At least that assured her that Tucker would remain with them at least a little longer. The problem was, as far as she was concerned, a little longer wasn't long enough.

When Claire and Tucker decided to come back to Paradise Ridge to celebrate their win, he had momentarily forgotten just how big Claire's family could be. Half her cousins and siblings had shown up for the last round of the finals, the other half seemed to be waiting here at the house for them.

Hiding out in the kitchen with Hazel cooking had been in his own self-defense. Not that he had a problem with anyone in her family, he was just terrified he'd do or say something stupid like blurt out his undying devotion in front of a full house. That alone wasn't a problem—he'd gladly shout his love for Claire from the highest mountain to be heard across the entire state of Texas. The problem was they hadn't had even five minutes alone to discuss anything, never mind how he felt about her. If he was going to be rejected, he'd rather it not be in front of an audience.

Now, whether he liked it or not, it seemed he was being backed into the proverbial corner.

"That's right," Claire spoke up. "Even though he is so much better, a long trailer ride to Wyoming on his feet would no doubt set him back."

He'd like to think that pitch was more for him than for his horse. "I'd hate to do that."

Claire leaned back in her chair. "There's time to decide what to do with the winnings."

"Have you considered land here in Texas?" Leah looked from Claire to Tucker.

"There ought to be a fair number of failed ranches that are available for sale." Cooper looked to Devlin for confirmation.

"But," Craig set his spoon down in his empty bowl, "those are hard to find. I remember when I was looking for studio land, that was no picnic. Harris County is wall to wall people and we own most of the land in Montgomery County. Unless you're thinking West Texas. Now out that way there's an awful lot of nothing available for the picking."

West Texas. Considering Texas was bigger than most European countries, he'd have rather had something a little closer to the reason he would even consider staying in Texas.

"It's a beautiful evening." Hazel popped her head in from the kitchen. "I put dessert out on the terrace. There's flan, blueberry crumb cake, and key lime pie."

"Key lime pie?" Siobhan pushed to her feet. "I'm on my way."

The sound of chairs scraping on the floor filled the room as one person after another pushed away from the table and made their way outside. Intentionally, Tucker took his time, hoping to pull Claire aside a minute, away from prying eyes.

Last in the line of relatives off to their share of a sugar rush, he snatched hold of Claire's hand and gently tugged her aside, away from the doorway and out of sight of the others.

Instantly, her eyes narrowed. "No sweets tonight?"

Curling her into the fold of his arms, he leaned down and placed a small and tender kiss on her lips, then rocking back on his heels, smiled down at her. "That's the only sweet thing I need."

Her shoulders relaxed and a smile bloomed. "Works for me."

Taking hold of her hands in each of his, he stared down at her. "There's something I need to know."

Their gazes fixed, she bobbed her head.

"Would you mind if I stayed in Texas?"

"Of course not," she answered without skipping a beat. A good sign as far as he was concerned.

Now came the harder part. "Would you like me to stay in Texas?"

Her expression softening, a hint of a smile teased her lips. "Very much."

Doing a fist pump and shouting hallelujah didn't seem appropriate at the moment, but inside he was silently dancing a celebratory jig. "We make a pretty good team, don't you think?"

"I'm amazed at how well the finals worked out." She chuckled softly. "I keep pinching myself to see if it really was me out there the last few days."

That wasn't exactly what he meant, but she had a point. "It was really you. I've never had a better partner."

"What about Sam?"

"Not even Sam." He shrugged. "Besides, I can't kiss him when we win."

That made her chuckle.

"Do you know how much I'd like to stay in Texas, close to you?"

Her gaze softened, and her voice lowered to match. "How much?"

Here it was. All or nothing. Reaching into his pocket, he

pulled out the tell-tale velvet box. Thanks to a little help from the Amore Cafe owner, he was able to get a really sweet deal on what he hoped was the perfect ring.

"Oh." Her mouth fell slightly open. The temptation to kiss away her surprise almost irresistible.

"I know I'm not rich like your family."

Provocative blue eyes glistened at him. "I don't care about money."

"And you know I would work every day of my life to make you happy."

She blinked and a single tear leaked from the corner of one eye. Lord, how he hoped that wasn't a bad sign.

Down on one knee, he hoped she could see all the love in his heart. "Claire Baron, I love you more than I thought ever possible, would you do me the honor, the absolute privilege, of being your husband?"

Another blink, another few leaky tears and her arms flung around his neck almost knocking him over. "Yes, yes, and oh, yes, I love you, too."

A whistle sounded from behind them as several family members applauded and Justin's younger brother Philip, shaking his head, cheekily sang out, *"And another one bites the dust."*

EPILOGUE

"**I**s it my imagination, or are we going to more charity balls and galas this year than in the last five years combined?" Facing his brother, Devlin fiddled with his tuxedo bow tie.

Oddly enough, though not quite the last five years, Cooper had been thinking more or less the same thing. After straightening his own tie, he double-checked that his cufflinks were tightly in place. A gift from his parents for his college graduation, the 22-karat gold Italian links with diamond initials had seemed absurd in his early twenties. Now, he treasured the gift.

The front door blew open and carrying a large garment bag in each arm, Mitch came through the front door, Gwyneth and the baby on his heels.

"Need some help?" Cooper leaped forward.

"Yeah. Help Gwen with the baby. I'll run these upstairs."

Devlin appeared at his side. "What's going on?"

Huffing from hurrying up the steps, Gwyneth smiled at her cousins-in-law. "Transformer blew. Half the city is in pitch black."

"I don't suppose," Devin checked his own cufflinks, "this means the evening is called off"?

She shook her head. "Nope. Downtown is well lit."

"Can't blame a man for asking." Devlin shrugged.

"I know how you feel." Gwyneth smiled at him. "Anyhow, the nanny was worried about her mother alone in the dark so we told her to go home."

"What about the baby?" Cooper stretched his hands out to the chubby little girl resting on her mother's hip, delighted when the sweet cherub flashed a toothless grin and flung herself toward him. "Atta girl. Come to Uncle Coop."

Her hands on her hips, Gwyneth shook her head. "You know, for a bachelor you're really good with babies."

Not till someone dropped newborn Beth in his arms had he ever thought of children as anything more than short people. Having something so delicate in his embrace, so dependent on him, and with a grip that could break a man's finger, she had completely won him over. He'd even found himself envying his cousins and siblings finding their own lifetime partners, and now starting families.

Dressed in a tuxedo, Tucker Pride, his sister Claire's fiancé, came in from the kitchen doorway. Shortly after winning the national rodeo championship and getting engaged to Claire, the Governor gave Claire one of the vacant houses on the property that had once belonged to one of Grams' bachelor uncles. For now, Tucker was working on the ranch and in his spare time, and on his insistence, with his own money, he'd been remodeling the old place for his bride-to-be. "Am I late?"

Cooper shook his head. "Grams and the Governor have not come down yet."

Glancing around the room, no doubt Tucker was looking for Claire.

"She's still upstairs," he informed his future brother-in-law.

Tucker bobbed his head, and glanced in the direction of the staircase. The longing in the guy's eyes actually made Cooper smile. Though longing might not have been the right word. The guy was so clearly in love with Claire that he looked as though he might die if he didn't see her soon.

"There's my girl." Wiping freshly washed hands on the hem of her apron, Hazel came from the kitchen, her hands extended in invitation.

Beth had reached an age where he would pay big bucks to know what thoughts were running around behind those pensive eyes. It took a few long moments, but finally the little girl decided that Hazel was not a foe and while she didn't throw herself the way she had with Cooper, she didn't object when the family cook pulled her away from him.

Another moment and Hazel and the baby disappeared at the top of the stairs at the same moment Claire appeared. He really had been blessed with three very smart and very beautiful sisters. He was delighted that Claire had found her perfect match; as they got older, he'd found himself worrying about his sisters more like a parent than a sibling. With the last about to be married, that was one load that seemed to roll off his shoulders. At least it would after the upcoming wedding.

Claire took a moment at the top of the stairs to scan the growing crowd in the foyer. Any fool could see the moment she spotted Tucker moving closer to the bottom of the stairs. Her smile bloomed and her eyes sparkled. If she were any more in love, her heart would probably beat right out of her chest. Slowly, she descended the stairway, her hand on the rail, her gaze never left Tucker.

"I swear those two are going to self-combust." Devlin chuckled from over his shoulder.

"All I know is things are getting awfully lovey-dovey around here all the time."

"Tell me about it." Devlin turned his wrist and checked his watch. "I'm going to head out and see how bad the blackouts are. Will report back."

Cooper bobbed his head. "Good idea."

His brother slapped him on the shoulder and when Cooper turned around, his sister had reached the bottom of the stairs. Gwyneth had waved on her way past Claire and up the stairs, but Claire had barely broken the connection with Tucker long enough to wave back. When Tucker extended his arm and she slipped her hand into his as she stepped into his personal space, Cooper would swear he'd never seen holding hands look so sensual in his life. When Tucker finally pulled her into his arms for a sweet, slow kiss, Cooper felt like a voyeur and turned away, giving them a little privacy. At least until his grandparents came out of their room.

Staring at the front door and debating if there was time for a drink before this show got on the road, Tucker and Claire stepped over beside him.

"Are you riding with us?" Tucker asked, holding Claire's hand.

"Not on your life."

"Excuse me?" Claire stared at him wide-eyed.

"You two enjoy dancing too much. As soon as we've put in a satisfactory appearance, I'm heading home to catch the end of the hockey game."

"Hockey? At this hour?" Claire blinked.

"Game is on the West Coast. If I don't get waylaid, I should be able to catch the third period. As a matter of fact, I'm going to head out now. The sooner I arrive, the sooner I can leave. I'm not sure if the Governor and Grams are going to ride with you, or Mitch, or if the new chauffeur is driving them."

"No problem." Tucker nodded, and slid his arm around Claire's waist. A casual, loving and protective gesture that Cooper was pleased to see, his sister was going to be very happy with this guy. "We can give them a ride and make sure they make it home too."

That was another thing about Tucker he liked. The man fit in with the Barons whether on a saddle or in a tuxedo, and he cared about Claire's entire family almost as much as he cared about Claire. All in all, his sisters had been blessed with their love lives. Too bad he couldn't say the same thing about himself.

"How did it go?" Cooper Baron's assistant Katrina crossed into his office.

"Same as always. I present the city with perfectly detailed plans and they want more."

Chuckling softly, Katrina shook her head. "Like you didn't know that was going to happen."

The woman was right. He'd been overly optimistic when he submitted the plans for the permits. "After all, I've only helped Rachel gut and rebuild more houses than the pencil pushers at city could count on all their hands and feet."

"I know." She crossed her arms. "How bad is it?"

He shook his head. "Not terribly. They want an additional cross beam. I know it's not needed. You know it's not needed. And I suspect so does city hall, but nowadays it's all about CYA."

"We have become the most litigious society in the world."

"Lucky us." Tilting his drafting table another inch, he finished making the changes that city hall wanted. Thankfully, Rachel didn't have the demolition on her latest project scheduled to start for another couple of weeks. That would be plenty of time to get city hall on board. Things were much easier before Chuck Nelson retired. After more than a decade working together, they'd developed a streamlined rapport. Now it looked like Cooper was going to be starting all over.

It also struck him that in this case, his last name had worked as a strike against him. Every once in a while—

okay, more often than not—the Baron family named opened doors and cut through red tape. But every so often, the name stirred resentment in folks who felt life had come too easy to anyone with the Baron last name. He'd be an idiot to argue there weren't perks to being a Baron. The biggest perk had absolutely nothing to do with power or prestige and everything to do with the love and support of a very large family. Despite Baron Enterprises having its fingers in everything from hotel resorts and restaurant chains, to sports teams and venture projects, the family's best benefit was just that, family. Even though there were enough Baron grandchildren to form a small city, they all knew each other, played with each other, worked with each other, and loved each other. And more importantly, had each other's backs, no questions asked.

Of course, having a surly retired Marine for a grandfather posed its own challenges, but in the end, love and respect trumped it all.

"Any updates on the new project manager?" Katrina picked up a stack of folders from the outbox on his desk.

Yes, nowadays everything was electronic, but he believed in paper backups for almost everything. Probably his grandfather's fault. "Well, she hasn't changed her mind and run for the hills, if that's what you're asking."

"Last I heard she was either reporting for work this Thursday or next Monday."

He bobbed his head. "Right. Not sure if her replacement might need a few extra days of support to handle some upcoming deadline, Tess wasn't sure when she could start, but apparently, she will be able to start Thursday."

"Tess? I thought her name is Teresa?"

"Yeah." He couldn't stop the smile from crossing his lips at the memories of the strong willed, confident, and oh so stubborn sophomore who tutored him through Physics. One of the smartest kids he'd known. After being laid up with mono for over a month, he'd fallen woefully behind in classes and Physics was the only teacher that refused to give him a lick of assistance in catching up. Tess had come to the rescue. Though he had no idea if she still used that nickname. "Teresa. That's right."

Katrina nodded. "Also, Gibbs from the Dallas hotel has been blowing up voicemail. Something about a new concrete supplier."

Immediately, Cooper checked his cell phone. "Dang it." Somehow, he'd switched his new phone to silent no vibration. The list of people who had been calling or texting him had him scrolling frantically. Words like 'honeycomb' and 'cracks' had Cooper biting down hard on his back teeth. All indicators of sub-par concrete. "I'll call him now."

"You'll also want to call your grandfather."

Cooper blew out a sigh. "Did Gibbs reach out to the Governor?"

Lips pressed tightly, clutching the folders to her chest, Katrina bobbed her head.

"Great. I'll call Gibbs first, then the Governor." And then he'd deal with the other texts pinging his phone. No matter what else was going on, this just became a priority. Nothing with the Baron name attached to it will be ever be done by cutting corners to save money. Nothing. Not. Ever. That was not, nor would it ever be, the Baron way.

"Knock knock." One of Tessa Gordon's associates rapped on the non-existent door of her corner cubicle.

That was just one of the small things she was looking forward to in her new job, a real office with a real door. "Hey, come on in."

Smiling, Nancy strolled in and came to a stop by Tessa's nearly empty desk. "Looks like you're almost done packing."

"Pretty much." Officially, yesterday had been her last day, but she'd opted to come in today to pack the rest of her things, just in case her replacement had any last minute questions. So far, the replacement seemed to be more than efficient enough.

"Remember, if there's a spot for me at Baron

Enterprises, don't forget your friend."

"You know I won't." Fully aware that she was the object of envy for many of the people in her office, she actually liked working with Nancy and wouldn't mind having that privilege again.

"I'll hold you to that. Especially after Ken and I start a family. Baron Enterprises is the most family friendly outfit in Texas. My sister's friend is an admin with one of their subsidiaries and she got sixty days paid leave before her due date and another ninety days after the baby. And then, having daycare in the building, she was able to keep nursing."

Tessa nodded. That was just one of the many reasons she jumped at the chance to apply for a project management position with the Barons. Having Emma nearby would do wonders to ease her guilt at having to work for a living. Not worrying about taking time off when she got sick—not that she got sick that often—but knowing that her job was secure even if she put her daughter first was huge for her. Having a chance to work with the Barons again was just as sweet a part of the deal. Tutoring Cooper Baron all those years ago had allowed her to visit the ranch and meet a good number of the family. She really loved his grandmother; a nicer woman did not exist. Once she got past the Governor's military demeanor, she found comfort in the frequent sparkle in the old man's eyes.

"Taking this?" Nancy held up Tessa's Employee of the Year award from a few years ago.

"Might be the only award I ever get." She took it from her friend and put it in the box with her other desktop items. How much would get unpacked was debatable, and she was very unlikely to display the thing at Barons. Did Barons even give out awards? Not that it mattered. While she'd definitely give her all to the job, there was a lot less 'all' available since she had Emma. She needed to keep perspective.

Checking the drawers one last time, then scanning the room, she wrapped her arms around the small box and straightened.

"So this is really it?" Nancy almost looked ready to cry.

"It's not like I'm moving to Bora Bora."

"At least if you were I'd have a good reason to visit."

The two women laughed.

"Spring is not that far away. We can still meet for lunch or dinner some time. If you're willing to drive to the burbs?"

"You bet. Who knows, maybe I'll give up my cute condo and trade it in for a little house with a yard, and stray cats, and a lawnmower, and…" Letting her gaze drift off somewhere beyond the window view, Nancy shook her head. "Or better yet, I'll drive to have lunch or dinner."

"There you go." Walking down the hall, Tessa shifted the box to one hip the way she might carry her daughter, freeing a hand to wave back at a few people before reaching the elevator.

Inside, the trip down seemed slower than usual. She'd been excited about the possibilities with her new job, but right now, thinking about all the changes coming to her and Emma's world, she couldn't stop smiling. Life was definitely looking up.

Read more of Just One Surprise available now

MEET CHRIS

USA TODAY Bestselling Author of dozens of contemporary novels, including the award winning Aloha Series, Chris Keniston lives in suburban Dallas with her husband, two human children, and two canine children. Though she loves her puppies equally, she admits being especially attached to her German Shepherd rescue. After all, even dogs deserve a happily ever after.

More on Chris and all her books can be found at
www.chriskeniston.com

Follow Chris' Monday Blog at her website
ChrisKenistonAuthor

Follow Chris on Facebook at
ChrisKenistonAuthor

Never miss a New Release!
Sign up for News from Chris:
www.chriskeniston.com/newsletter.html

Questions? Comments?
I would love to hear from you! You can reach me at:
chris@chriskeniston.com